A FIELD GUIDE TO THE ALIENS OF

STAR TREK

THE NEXT GENERATION

BY JOSHUA CHAPMAN

EDITED BY ZACHARY AUBURN

D1546425

THE
DEVASTATOR
LOS ANGELES

First Edition: September 2017

ISBN-13: 978-1-942099-28-4

ISBN-10: 1-942099-28-2

devastatorpress.com

PRINTED IN ~~THE RESORT PLANET OF RISA~~ KOREA

CONTENTS

I did not write the book you hold in your hands, but I could have.

In May of 2010, I was visiting a friend in Pittsburgh, Pennsylvania. We had decided to spend an afternoon going to garage sales, and it was there when I came across a box of old zines being sold for a dollar each. There was a lot of good stuff in that box: old issues of *Dishwasher and Burn Collector* and *Guinea Pig Zero*, but by far the greatest treasure was a set of six dog-eared zines bound together by a decaying rubber band. Six zines that, based on the (incorrectly spelled) "copywrite" dates on the back cover, had been penned one per year over the course of the first half of the nineties. Written across the cover in appallingly messy cursive was the title, *A Field Guide to the Aliens of Star Trek: The Next Generation.* By Joshua Chapman, Grade Seven.

I fell in love with these zines. More than just teaching me the difference between the Takarans, Talarians and the Tamarians, they provided a window into Joshua's unhappy adolescence, and his growing obsession with the show that allowed him to escape it. I loved his fixation on Data, his frustration with Troi, and his amazement at the number of aliens in the universe who bore an uncanny resemblance to humans. But mostly I loved how, without realizing it (at least at first) the author used his love of Star Trek to talk about things that he otherwise had no way of saying. It was sad and weird and funny in a way that held a mirror up to much of my own adolescence. Like I said, I did not write this book, but I could have.

When I returned home, I resolved to find out as much as I could about the zines and their author, only to discover... nothing. No one I asked had ever heard of the zines. Joshua Chapman was too generic a name for Google to be of any assistance in tracking him down, and the zines were too old and too obscure to ever have been mentioned online.

Nevertheless, Joshua's work was too wonderful to let it molder in obscurity. I spent years dreaming of compiling the zines into a book. I thought they were great, and I wanted more people to experience the same thrill I did when I first discovered them. But I never felt comfortable proceeding without the involvement of Joshua. I spent four years attempting to track down Joshua without success... until now. Last fall, I found someone who worked in one of the few record stores that originally sold the zines. He was able to tell me the high school Joshua attended, and from there it was easy to discover his current whereabouts and get in touch with him.

I am ecstatic to say that not only did Joshua give his blessing to collect his zines into a book, but he was also kind enough to sit for a short interview, as well as come out of retirement to provide entries for the six alien races that appeared in the *Star Trek: The Next Generations* movies and the four aliens he missed on the TV show! I will be forever grateful to Joshua for what he has created, and I say to him from the bottom of my heart: Live long and prosper.

ZACHARY AUBURN

SEASON ONE

FIRST PUBLISHED: 1990
AUTHOR AGE: 11

Joshua Chapman   May 15, 1990
English   Grade 7

A Field Guide

to the Aliens of

Season
One

Introduction

For my creative writng project I decided to write a guide to all the aliens on the tv show Star Trek: The Next Generation. I think that this is the best show on tv, and I think people would benefit from knowing about the aliens that appeared on this show. I hope you find this guide interesting and useful.

Aliens

of the

Enterprise

Betazoids

Home Planet:
Betazed
Episode:
all
Rating: ✭✭

We don't get to see these aliens too much, (other than Counsellor Troi and her mom), or find out a lot about them. They have naked weddings I guess, which seems like a bad idea. If I was getting married in a Betazoid wedding I would be really worried because everyone would be looking at me, but there would be lots of naked women there, and I might get an erection. It is like an even worse version of the nightmare where you are in school in your underpants.

The big deal with Betazoids is that they are psychic, which seems like it would make them cool, but

they are mostly just annoying.
Counsellor Troi is half-Betazoid,
which means that she can sense
emotions, but mostly she just says
things that they know already, plus
she is really weak and spends a lot
of time looking like she has a
headache. Half the time it is like
she is about to start crying. I
dont know how the other people on
the ship can deal with it. Her mom
is a full Betazoid, and she is
really annoying and pushy. There
might be other Betazoids out there
who are not annoying, and use
their powers in interesting ways,
but if so we dont see them

Data

Home Planet:
Omicron Theta
Episode:
all
Rating: ✭✭✭✭✭

Data is not really an alien, he is
a humanoid android, but I am
going to write about him anyway
because he is basically the best
person on the ship. Here are some
of the reasons Data is great:

1: He is really smart. His brain
is basically a computer. He can
read really fast and when he learns
something he can remember it
forever. Whenever they need to know
anything, Data is the person they

ask. I think I am like Data in that way.

2: He is incredibly fast. There was an episode where part of a star that exploded was going to crash into the ship, but the computer was broken and Data was the only person who could fix it in time. His hands moved so fast you could barely see them. Another thing that happened in that episode is that him and Tasha Yar had sex. I have never had a girlfriend but I think Tasha Yar would be a good one. She is definitely more pretty than Troi or Dr Crusher. They were only together once but I think they still cared about each other a lot, and sometimes after Tasha died Data would look at a hologram of her. I wish they had been a couple, but I dont know much about relationships so maybe it would be a bad idea. A few weeks ago some of the guys at school told me there was a girl in my class who thought I was cute, and asked me if I wanted to know who it was. I figured they were probably trying to play a trick on me so I told them no. Then they asked what was wrong with me if I didnt want a girlfriend. I told them I didnt need a girlfriend because I had video games, and then they made fun of me.

But then later on I found out
that the girl who thought I
was cute was Amanda, and I
am fine not dating her because
she looks like the type of
person who might smoke cigarettes.
3: He is really strong, probably
way stronger than Worf, but
unlike Klingons he doesn't talk
about it all the time. Data is
really humble and I respect that.

The other thing about Data is
that he doesn't have any emotions
so human behavior doesn't make
a lot of sense to him. He is
always trying to learn how to
be more human, but I think
he is better off without emotions.

Klingons

Home Planet:
Kronos
Episode:
all
Rating: ★★★

Worf is okay, but most of these aliens seem like jerks. All they do is fight and push people around. They are basically bullies, but in outer space. They remind me a lot of some of the guys at school who are always pushing people around. Klingons always talk about how great they are. They talk about being brave and honorable and that they are great warriors all the time. The thing is, Klingons think they are ~~strong~~ and powerful, but Data is way stronger than them.

Aliens not
of the
Enterprise

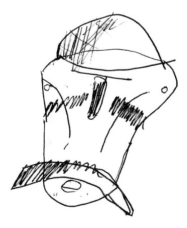

Bandi

Home Planet:
Deneb IV
Episode:
Encounter at Farpoint
Rating: ✗✗

These guys look like humans, but they are not. If you ever meet a Bandi, you should not trust them. In the first episode they promised the Federation that they would build them a Starbase, but then instead they captured a space jellyfish and enslaved it, which is pretty much the jerkiest thing you can do. You only really get to meet the leader of these people, but if he is any indication they are not to be trusted.

Q

Home Planet:
?
Episode:
Encounter at Farpoint
Rating: ✗ ✗ ✗ ✗

Q is a guy who basically has godlike powers. All he has to do is think something, and then it happens. Most of the time this just means making people wear silly clothing, but sometimes he throws the Enterprise accross the Galaxy. A lot of the time Q acts like a jerk, but I also kind of like him. He picks on people, but it seems like the ones he picks on are the ones who are full of themselves.

Space Jellyfish

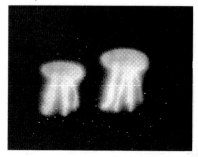

Home Planet:
?
Episode:
Encounter at Farpoint
Rating: ✗✗✗✗

These things are incredible! They are huge, like ten times the size of the Enterprise. And they look like jellyfish! They are a special kind of lifeform which can live in outer space and doesn't need a ship, because they are sort of like ships already. Also, they have psychic powers, but not in the lame Betazoid way. They can make things appear just by thinking about them. You just have to say what you want, and these things make it appear. They are pretty clever. They do this a few times so the Enterprise will know something fishy is going on, but it probably would have been an even better idea if instead of making some fancy cloth or bowls of apples if they made a note that explained what was happening.

We see two of them, and I guess they are supposed to be dating, or married or something. Whatever it is that jellyfish do. One of them has been captured, and the other comes and kills the people who captured it, which is really romantic. I think it is sweet that they care about each other that much.

Ligonians

Home Planet:
Ligon II
Episode:
Code of Honor
Rating: ☆

These guys are awful. They dont look cool at all, they just look like normal humans. They treat women bad. They talk about honor all the time but they act like jerks. I think the writers of this show must not like honor, because any time aliens talk about how honor is super important to them, you know they are going to act like jerks.

I also think it's wierd that they made these guys black. I mean, I think it's fine that there are black aliens. But they walk around like they are characters from some

really old racist cartoon. They
wear turbans and puffy pants
and I don't see why they
didn't just go all the way
and have them constantly
walking around holding watermelons
or something.

Ferengi

Home Planet:
Ferenginar
Episode:
The Last Outpost
Rating: ☆ ☆

I don't get these aliens at all. They seem really dumb, and all they care about is making money, and they are very mean and cowardly. On the other hand, they get bonus points because they don't just look like humans. I don't understand why so many aliens look just like humans. But the Ferengi have giant foreheads and giant ears.

Tau Alpha Cetans

Home Planet:
Tau Alpha C
Episode:
Where No One Has Gone Before
Rating: ★★★★

We only ever meet one of these aliens. He calls himself the Traveller and he can manipulate warp fi lds with his mind. These aliens have figured out that space and time and thought are all connected, and he can manipulate reality just by thinking abord it. This makes a lot of sense, because if you look at his hands, they look really clumsy. He just has three giant weird fingers, and I bet because these aliens are not good at holding things that they had to develop their psychic abilities

Energy Cloud Aliens

Home Planet:
?

Episode:
Lonely Among Us
Rating: ☆ ☆

In one episode the Enterprise flies
through a nebula and one of these
aliens accidentally gets trapped
on the ship and takes control of
Worf. Then later it takes control
of Doctor Crusher and Captain Picard.
At first the alien seems like it is
being mean on purpose, but maybe
it was just confused, and didn't
really understand what humans were.
I think it would be cool to have
the powers that these aliens have.
They can just fly around and go
whereever they want, but if they

need to talk to somebody they can just take over someones body. This seems like a really useful ability. If someone was trying to beat you up they couldnt because you dont have a body. And if you were in a body, you could just leave that body, or maybe even take over the body of the person who was trying to beat you up. I think that would be a good trick. One time in math class I got a D on a test and I almost started crying, but it wasnt my fault because I hadnt slept well the night before the test, and Kevin started making fun of me and called me a crybaby But if I was like the Energy Cloud aliens I could take over his body every time he took a test, and make him get every answer wrong.

Anticans

Home Planet:
Antica
Episode:
Lonely Among Us
Rating: ✫✫

I guess these guys are supposed to be dog aliens. I am not a big fan of dogs because when I was a kid a dog attacked me. I think cats are way better. My cat right now is named Socks. She sleeps in my bed at night and keeps me company. I dont know why but she really likes licking my hair. Sometimes she wakes me up that way. When she does it she purrs a lot. When I am feeling sad I will put her on my bed and lay down next to her and she will lick my hair for like half an hour. It makes me feel better

when she does this because it is
nice to get attention and it is like
giving me attention is the most
enjoyable feeling in the world for
her and that is a really nice feeling
to know she loves me that much.
Anyways, these guys are the enemies
of the Selay aliens

Selay

Home Planet:
Selay
Episode:
Lonely Among Us
Rating: ✗ ✗

These are lizard aliens, and they
are the enemies of the dog-like
Anticans. It was the Enterprise's
job to take these guys to some
negotiations. Both of these races hate
each other for basically no reason.
I guess the show was trying to
make a point about how war is
dumb, and it is stupid to hate
someone just because they are different than you. But when one of
the Selay is killed by the
Anticans, the Enterprise crew

basically says, "Whoops! Oh well!" like it is no big deal that someone was just murdered on their ship. I feel like this show does that a lot. They talk about how everyone is equal, but they make it like Humans are better than anyone else.

Edo

Home Planet:
Edo
Episode:
Justice
Rating: ★ ★

These people make me uncomfortable.
They wear almost no clothing and
are constantly talking about sex. I
dont see how they managed to build
a bunch of buildings and fountains
when all they do is run around
and kiss and give each other back
rubs. They seem kind of like stupid
children, because they believe that a
spaceship is a god. also, they have
really strict laws, and the only
punishment for breaking the law
is death. I definitely wouldn't

want to live on this planet.
Everyone who lives there is
really beautiful and perfect-looking,
but they are also kind of jerks
for wanting to kill Wesley even
though it was just a mistake.
But that is also sort of just
like real life because the most
popular kids at school are also the
meanest, and they are dumb
like the Edo are too.

Dods of Edo

Home Planet:
Edo
Episode:
Justice
Rating: ✸ ✸

There is a thing above the planet the
Edo live on that is sort of like a
spaceship, but also it is a group of
aliens, but also it coexists in several
dimensions. They are pretty confusing
aliens. Even though they can exist as
balls of energy I think they are
not very smart, because they keep
the Edo as pets, and the Edo are
dumb. It would be like if someone
had an annoying dog as a pet.
There is probably something wrong
with that person, or else they would
just get a cat instead. That is another
reason Data is great, he has a pet cat.
Even though Data doesn't have
emotions I can tell he loves his cat.

Jarada

?

Home Planet:
Torona IV
Episode:
The Big Goodbye

These aliens are supposed to look like giants bugs, which makes it a tragedy that we never get to see them, because I bet they look cool. They think rules and protocol are the most important things. Picard is supposed to deliver a greeting to them, and if he mispronounces any word it will mean a disaster. The thing I dont understand is why they dont just get Data to do it. Another thing that Data can do is replicate anyones voice, and the Jarada would never know the difference.

Tarellians

Home Planet:
Tarella
Episode:
Haven
Rating: ✗✗✗

A few hundred ~~years~~ ago, these aliens had a horrible civil war where they used biological warfare on each other, and they created a horrible plague that wiped out most of their species. Then they tried to escape their planet, but they took ~~their~~ plague with them, and they started infecting other planets too. So all the aliens in the galaxy would destroy Tarellian ships on sight so ~~they~~ wouldn't risk being infected. But I don't understand how if the plague is so bad that there are still Tarellians wandering around hundreds of years later. Shouldn't the plague have killed them all off? Also, these aliens always wear blue and purple clothes, and I guess they are psychic because one of the women made some human guy draw pictures of her even though he was light years away.

Crystaline Entity

Home Planet:
?

Episode:
Datalore
Rating: ✦✦

This is a giant snowflake that kills people. Data's evil brother Lore is friend with it, and uses it to kill people he doesn't like. Lore used it to kill all the people on the planet they came from. This is why I think it is a good idea to not have emotions. Data doesn't have any and he is great.

But Lore has emotions and it makes him crazy. The Crystaline Entity is way bigger than the Enterprise, but it can't get through the shields. However it can use a beam or something to strip all the living matter from a planet.

Angellians

Home Planet:
Angel One
Episode:
Angel One
Rating: ✗✗

This is another race of aliens that look exactly like humans, plus apparently humans and them can have babies. This seems like an amazing coincidence. I dont understand why people on Star Trek arent more curious about why there are so many aliens that look just like them, but not Klingons, or Romulans, or anyone else.

Binar

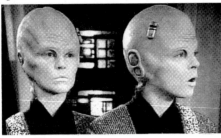

Home Planet:
Binar
Episode:
1100100l
Rating: ✗✗✗✗

These guys are pretty cool. They get bonus points for not looking just like humans. They are purple and short and talk to each other in binary and they think like computers. They only work in pairs, because this is more efficent for them. Their brains are tied to a giant computer, but they are worried the sun is going to explode so they steal the Enterprise so they can store their brains on that instead. I think this would be a good thing to be able to do because then you could just put all the bad stuff that happens to you onto a computer and delete it.

Aldeans

Home Planet:
Aldea
Episode:
When the bough
breaks
Rating: ✗✗

These are super-smart aliens
who decided that they wanted nothing
to do with the rest of the universe, so they put a cloaking
device on their planet so they
could hang out and make art
all the time. But then their
cloaking device gave them radiation
poisoning and they couldn't have
children, so they decided to kidnap
some kids off the Enterprise. Which
is weird. These aliens look human,
but they're not human. Why do
they care about kids who are
from a different species. And

there are a lot of other aliens out there who look human. So why not find some aliens who dont care about their kids very much and kidnap them instead? Also, the place they live looks really boring. No one ever goes outside, and for people who have spent thousands of years making art, their apartments are really boring. They dont even have any paintings on their walls.

Microbrain

Home Planet:
Velara III
Episode:
Home Soil
Rating: ✗✗

These are tiny crstal lifeforms
that have a hive mind. They live
in the sand, and sometimes form
geometric patterns in it for some
reason. They are really upset at
Star Fleet for trying to kill them.
The people on the Enterprise seem
really surprised that there could be
an inorganic life form, even though
they just met a giant murdering
crystal who kills entire planets.

So I dont see what the big deal is. They kill one of the Star Fleet guys, but I can kind of understand that. If someone hurts you over and over again you are going to start to hate them, even if they dont mean to hurt you. The Star Fleet guys should have been more careful.

Vulcans

Home Planet:
Vulcan
Episode:
Coming of Age
Rating: ✱✱✱✱✰

I think that Star Trek: The Next Generation is way better than the old Star Trek. The special effects on the old Star Trek just weren't very good. But the one good thing about the original show is Spock, who is a Vulcan. Vulcans are a lot like Data. They are really smart and really strong, and they are very unemotinional. Here is the thing: they have psychic powers. The Betazoids are psychic, but

they are horrible. All they ever
do is whine and cry and look
like they have to B.M. and I
dont understand why they
are so awful. And the Vulcans
prove that if you dont have
so many emotions you would
be like a thousand times
better.

Zaldan

Home Planet:
?

Episode:
Coming of Age

Rating: ✷✷

These guys look like humans except
that they have webbed hands, which
is pretty weird. They hate it when
people are polite to them because they
think the persons behavior is dishonest, but that doesn't really make
sense to me because when Wesley
bumps into them in the hall he
is dishonest when he pretends to
be angry, and then the Zaldan guy
is okay with that. I don't understand why people would get mad
if you try to be polite. These
guys are an excellent example of

why emotions are dumb and confusing. My mom is always sad in the morning and cries for a really long time, but when I try to make her feel better she starts yelling and leaves the room and starts slamming doors. If being nice is just going to make someone act worse, then we are definitely better off not having emotions, like Data

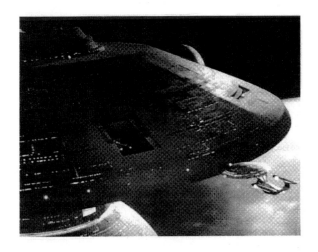

Benzite

Home Planet:
Benzar
Episode:
Coming of Age
Rating: ✗ ✗ ✗

These aliens are blue, and they
have weird faces, and they need
a special device to breathe because
normal human air is not enough
for them, and if they just
breathed that they would suffocate.
I think that would be weird.
To have air you could breathe in
and out, but you still suffocated?
I think drowning would be really
scary because I dont like swimming,
but suffocating actually seems
like it would be peaceful.

Sometimes in the morning when my mom is downstairs and screaming and slamming doors I will lay in my bed and push my pillow against my face so I cant breathe until I start to feel dizzy, and then when I am done I am not as scared as I was. I dont want to suffocate, but I think it would probably be a lot better than having your airplane explode, or being eaten by a shark.

Ornarans & Brekkians

Home Planet:
Ornara + Brekka
Episode:
Symbiosis
Ratng: ✗✗✗/✗✗

These aliens share a solar system.
The Ornarans spent all of their
energy developing technology, while
the Brekkians worked on learning
how to be drug dealers. At first
you think the Ornarans are stupid
because they dont know how to
repair their ship, but it is just that
they are drug addicts. And the
Brekkians seem like huge jerks.
They are super snotty and stuck-up.
Even though the Ornarans use drugs,
by the end of the episode you find
out that they are the good guys.

Armus

Home Planet: Vagra II
Episode: Skin of Evil
Rating: ✗

This guy is the worst alien on Star Trek. He is horrible. He is evil and mean and he looks stupid and I hate him so much. He killed Tasha for no reason. Its not fair. At the end of the episode the Enterprise just flies away but I would have blown up the planet with photon torpedos. He is so powerful and it is not fair that he took Tasha away from Data and there is nothing they could do about it. I hate him I hate him I hate him.

Conspiracy Aliens

Home Planet:
?
Episode:
Conspiracy
Rating: ✹ ✹

We never find out the name
of these aliens, but they are pretty
weird. They are small, and they
look like a crayfish, and they
crawl into peoples mouths and take
control of their brains. Once the
alien is in control of you, you
have super strength, but the
alien is in control of your body,
and it cant use your memories.
At one point these aliens say
that they love the theatre, which

is weird. Does that mean on
their planet they have little
crayfish theatres? Because all
you ever see these aliens do is
try to take over the Federation,
it is hard to imagine them going
to plays. The leader of the aliens
lived in the guy who plays
Geoge Frankly on Mathnet,
which is cool, because I loved
that show. It was definitely
my favorite part of Square One.

Romulans

Home Planet:
Romulus
Episode:
The Neutral Zone
Rating: ✱ ✱ ✱

The Romulans are sort of like Vulcans, except that they have emotions and are really sneaky. That is the main thing about them, is that they are smart, but not very trustworthy, and also their ships are cool looking.

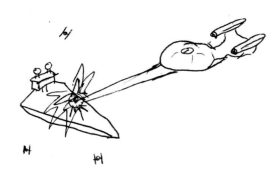

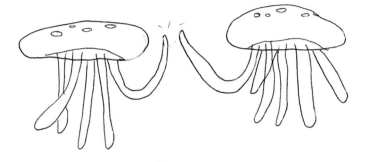

SEASON TWO

FIRST PUBLISHED: 1991
AUTHOR AGE: 12

Joshua Chapman

English - Extra Credit

April 13, 1991

Grade 8

A Field Guide to the Aliens of

Season Two

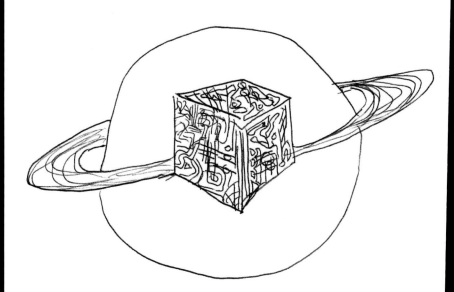

Introduction

Welcome to the second part of my guide to
the aliens of Star Trek: The Next Generation. I did the first one last year for
an assignment in my English class. We
don't have an assignment like that this
year, but my school counselor said that
she really likes Star Trek, and that she
thought the first one was really interesting, and that she hoped I would write
another. So she arranged for me to get
extra credit for writing this. Which is
pretty cool. This season has way less
aliens than last season, partly because
some of the aliens are just repeats of
ones we have seen before, and partly because there are a bunch of episodes that
are just dealing with dumb things like
a virus that makes you old or a planet
of Irish people. Even thought there are
fewer aliens, there are still some really good ones, and I hope you enjoy this
guide.

Guinan

Home Planet: ?
Episode: The Child
Rating: ××××

We don't know the name of the aliens that Guinan is from, but they seem pretty interesting! Guinan is really old, at least hundreds of years old. Her race were almost wiped out by the Borg, and at one point she fought with Q, which is pretty impressive. Guinan is very mysterious, but she always seems to have good advice for people, and she is really smart. It's funny, because even though she doesn't have telepathic powers she is much better at helping people with their problems than Counsellor Troi.

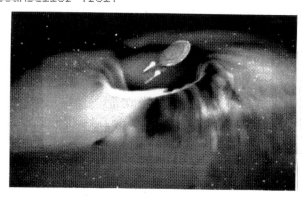

Lifeforce Entity

Home Planet : ?
Episode: The Child
Rating ˣ

These are pretty stupid aliens. These aliens look like Tinkerbell, and they raped Counsellor Troi in her sleep. And then it got her pregnant with itself. Counsellor Troi is always annoying, but in this episode she is annoying and really crazy. First the alien makes her crazy by forcing her to hear its heartbeat when it is still a fetus. Then when it is born it grows really fast, and Troi acts like nothing at all is weird even though she has an alien baby that is growing really fast. No one knows why the alien is there and Troi acts like it is not a big deal, but if I was a girl and an alien got me pregnant I would want to know why it did that.

Negilum

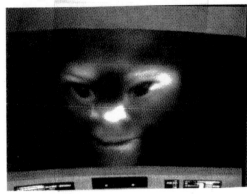

Home Planet: ?
Episode: Where
Silence Has Lease
Rating: **

Negilum is a lot like Q. They are both incredibly powerful beings who are curious about humans and perform experiments on them. The difference is that Q is sort of funny, but Negilum is a jerk who murders people for no reason and has a weird face. The strangest part about his face is that he says he went to a lot of effort to look like humans, except that he doesn't really look like humans, and it didn't seem to be a lot of effort for him to trap the Enterprise in an infinite void, or create fake starships, or create fake versions of Troi and Data. So it is confusing that it would be hard for him to give himself a face. That seems like a much easier thing to do.

The Coalition of Madena

Home Planet: Altec and Straleb
Episode: The Outrageous Okona
Rating: ×××

These aliens live on two different planets. The main thing about them is one of these aliens is named Captain Okana, and he is basically the Star Trek version of Han Solo. Some of the kids at school say that Star Wars is better than Star Trek, but they are definitely crazy. Think about it this way: What would happen if a Star Destroyer had to fight the Enterprise? The Enterprise would definitely win. The Star Destroyer has lots of TIE fighters, but they don't even have shields, they would die right away. And in Return of the Jedi they destroy a Super Star Destroyer basically just by crashing an A-Wing into the bridge! They are the smallest kind of ship, and it still destroyed them!. There is no way a Star Destroyer would have a chance. Plus the Star Destroyers still use lasers, which are not as powerful as phasers. Just like the Enterprise is better than a Star Destroyer, Star Trek is definitely better than Star Wars.

Solari

Home Planet:
Solais V
Episode: Loud
as a Whisper
Rating: ˣˣ

These are aliens who have been fighting amongst themselves for a really long time, to the point where they are almost extinct. They are sort of dirty looking, and they have messy hair, and their faces are really puffy like they have been stung by giant bees. I don't really understand why they are still fighting. It looks like their planet is pretty crappy. It's the future. They have spaceships, and there are a bunch of uninhabited planets that are probably much nicer than theirs. I don't see why one of the groups doesn't just get in a spaceship and say "So long" and go live someplace nicer.

Ramanti

Home Planet:
Ramatis III
Episode: Loud
as a Whisper
Rating: ˣ ˣ ˣ

These are human looking aliens. We meet them when one of their leaders comes aboard the Enterprise. He is a famous negotiator, and he is deaf, and he has three people who read his thoughts and communicate for him. Which seems like a really crappy job. You have to spend your entire life following some guy around and telling people what he is thinking because he cannot be bothered to write down what he wants people to know. Everyone on the show keeps talking about what a good negotiator he is, but I am not so sure. It seems like he is only really interested in making out with Counsellor Troi, and he gets annoyed whenever anyone suggests that he do some negotiating instead of putting the moves on her.

Allasamorphs

Home Planet:
Daled IV
Episode: The
Dauphin
Rating ××××

These aliens are shape shifters, which is one
of the best abilities an alien can have. Tele-
kinesis would also be a good ability. Invisibility would be good too, although I guess these
aliens could just change into an invisible creature, like the Predator, and then you could have
both abilities. When these aliens are in their
natural state they look sort of like the inside
of a lava lamp, but at other times they also will
look like teddy bears, or Wookies, or beautiful
women. One of them falls in love with Wesley,
which is sort of dumb. Partially because of how
pretty she is, I don't think she would like a guy
like Wesley. But also because Wesley is a jerk
to her. The world these aliens come from have
been at war for an incredibly long time, and she
is the key to peace between the two sides. Wesley keeps on telling her that she can do whatever

she wants but that is not true. Most of the time
we can't. Maybe Wesley can because he lives on
the Enterprise, but in the real world we are stuck
with what our life is. The alien has people that
she needs to take care of and Wesley is a jerk for
trying to make her think she can walk away from
that, because she can't.

Iconians

Home Planet: Iconia
Episode: Contagion
Rating ˣˣˣ

People called these aliens "demons of air and
darkness" which is definitely the coolest descrip-
tion of an alien we have ever heard on Star Trek.
It makes them sound like a Balrog, which is awesome. The Iconians lived hundreds and thousands
of years ago. They had magic portals that allowed
them to teleport to other places. This seems like
a really useful invention. I hate taking the bus
to school in the morning because every day on the
way to school I feel sick to my stomach, but if I
had one of these I wouldn't have to ride the bus
at all. I could just sit at home playing with
Legos until right before class, then just jump
through the portal and I would be there instantly.

Dremans

Home Planet:
Drema IV
Episode Pen
Pals
Rating ×××

These aliens are short, with orange skin and long fingers and it sort of looks like they are covered with glitter. The planet that they lived on was going to be destroyed because of volcanos, but there was a little girl who had a radio and she contacted Data and they became friends. Then Data saved them because he was the only one brave enough to violate the prime directive. Afterwards they had to wipe the girls memory. I am not sure how I feel about this. There have been lots of times when things are bad with my mom that I have wished that Star Trek was real, and imagined if maybe there was a transporter malfunction and they accidentally beamed me up. If this happened I would never tell anyone about it. I don't think there is anything in the universe that would make me happier than getting to go on the Enterprise, and I would have no problem keeping it a secret so they wouldn't have to erase my memory. The planet that this alien girl lives on was saved, but I am sure it was still really badly damaged by the volcanos. I am sure she has a very hard life ahead of her, and it would be nice if she had a good memory to hold onto, like getting to meet Data.

Borg

Home Planet:
?
Episode Q-
Who
Rating ×××××

The Borg are AWESOME. They are aliens
who look like humans with robotic parts attached. They are definitely the best looking
aliens that have ever been on Star Trek. They
have a hive mind, which makes them really smart.
They are also very strong, and good at adapt-
ing. Their ship is huge, and it is way more powerful than the Enterprise, and faster than it
too. I wouldn't necessarily want to be a Borg,
because then I would lose my personality, but I
still think these aliens kick butt. The Enterprise meets these aliens because Q thinks that
humans have gotten too cocky, so this episode
has a good moral too, because the Federation is
sort of like the popular kids at school, and they
think they're the best but then the Borg comes
and shows them that they are way more powerful.

Pakleds

Home Planet:?
Episodes:
Samatarian
Snare
Rating: *

I hate these aliens. They are fat and ugly and they look stupid. Not only do they look stupid, they are stupid too. They are basically space bullies, and they steal from people who are smarter and nicer than they are. The Pakleds kidnap Geordi, and the Enterprise has to trick them so they can get Geordi back. But I wish the Enterprise would have just shot their ship with phasers until the shields dropped and then teleported Geordi back, and then blown up their ship with photon torpedos. If they are going to be that stupid and mean, that is what they deserve. Awhile ago some kids at school were bullying me, and I tried to hit one of them and I accidentally scratched their cornea, and I was the one who got in trouble! That is so dumb! They even threatened to kick me out of school but that is bullsht. What I did was an accident but they were the

ones who started it. If anything they should
get kicked out of school, not me. This is why
I think the Enterprise should have blown up
their ship. If you are going to bully people,
you deserve whatever happens to you.

Antedeans

Home Planet:
Antede III
Episode: Man-
hunt
Rating ××

These are weird fish aliens. They have blue skin and bulging eyes on the side of their head and are really ugly. Worf keeps talking about how they are really handsome, but I am not sure I believe him. Maybe he is telling the truth, because Klingons are also strange looking. But in my experience when lots of kids tell you that you are funny looking and then someone tells you that they think you're attractive, that person is probably trying to trick you.

Zakdorn

Home Planet: ?
Episode: Peak
Performance
Rating: × × × ×

These aliens are weird. They look sort
of like pigs with melted faces stuck on Humpty
Dumpty bodies. They are very rude and insulting to people On the other hand, they are very
good at games, and I respect that. People say
that they are the most brilliant strategists in
the galaxy, although when the Zakdorn guy chal-
lenges Data to Stratagema Data still finds a way
to win. Even though I don't get to play games
against other people very much I think I am good
at games too. Last summer I got a game called
Stratego at a garage sale. I haven't played
anyone at it yet but I studied the rules and I
know I have figured out the best starting po-
sition, so when I do play someone at it I know
they will have no chance to beat me.

SEASON THREE

FIRST PUBLISHED: 1992
AUTHOR AGE: 13

A Field Guide
to the Aliens of

Season Three

a zine by Joshua Chapman

Introduction

This year I started a new school. The people here are way better than at my old school. I think the coolest person is this guy named Tristan. He is a senior and he is into some thing called "Cyberpunk", which basically means that he dresses sort of like a Borg. He writes these things called zines, which are like little magazines that he makes with the schools photocopier. They have stuff in them like reviews of music he likes, and stories, and in one issue he had a diagram of a molecule of acid (the drug). That is crazy. I don't know how he doesn't get arrested. Anyways, I like writing about Star Trek, so I decided that I am going to keep writing this, and it is going to be zine.

Sheliak

Home Planet: Shelia
Episode: The Ensigns of Command
Rating: ****

These aliens are like the goths of Star Trek. They are
cool looking and they are disdainful of other aliens and they
hang out in dark rooms. Most aliens on Star Trek basically
look like humans, but these things are crazy looking. It is
like a blob monster is wiggling around while wearing a blan-
ket with sparkles on it.

Douwd

Home Planet : ?
Episode: The Survivors
Rating ****

This alien is a badass. He has infinite powers like Q, but
he just wants to have a peaceful life, instead of going
around playing tricks on people. Then he finds out that
his wife died and he gets so pissed off that he kills all
the Husnock aliens. Not just the ones attacking his planet, but all the Husnock everywhere. Tristan, the guy at
my school, his favorite band is called Nine Inch Nails. I
really like them too. They have a song called "Something
I Can Never Have" that reminds me a lot of this episode.
Because the Douwd guy is sad that he committed genocide,
so he makes a fake version of his wife to help him forget
what he's done. The lyrics seem like they are almost exactly talking about this episode. I definitely think this
is their best song, it is really sad and pretty.

Husnock

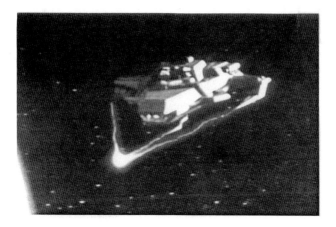

Home Planet: ?
Episode: The Survivors
Rating: **

These are aliens who used to go around the galaxy killing people. Then they killed the wife of a guy who had godlike powers,
so he erased them from existence. Which teaches us an important lesson: don't kill the wives of people with godlike powers,
because they can mess you up. We don't know a lot else about
them, because they are all dead before the episode even starts.

Mintakan

Home Planet: Mintaka III
Episode: Who Watches the Watchers
Rating: ***

In the episode they say that these aliens are proto Vulcan, and they do look like Vulcans, but it seems like the reason they say they are proto Vulcan is because they are super obsessed with logic and reason. Which is dumb, because everyone knows that early Vulcans were really emotional, and they didn't start liking logic until way later.

The Federation was studying these aliens, but then the hologram that hid their research post broke down, and then these aliens thought that Picard was god. Which is a dumb thing to think. Even when I was a little kid I didn't believe in God. My mom would make me go to mass on Christmas, and it was basically the most boring thing in the world. Religion is like sports, it is just something governments use to keep stupid people happy.

Menthar and Promellian

Home Planet: ?
Episode: Booby Trap
Rating: **

These are two alien races that killed each other off a thousand years ago. Picard makes a big deal out of how advanced
their ships were for the time period, even though there were
a lot of aliens flying around the galaxy back then so these
aliens actually aren't special at all. The Menthar aliens
set up a booby trap to capture the Promellian ship, where
the more the Promellians try to escape the more it drains
their energy. This sounds horrible to me. There is no feeling I hate more than being trapped. It is horrible. I used
to have nightmares about this, about struggling and not being able to move, and sometimes when I would wake up my mom
would be sitting at the end of my bed looking at me.

Barzan

Home Planet: Barzan II
Episode: The Price
Rating: ***

The universe gave these aliens sort of a bad deal. They live on
a crappy planet with no resources that is poisonous for other
people to visit, and they are dependent on other aliens help to
survive. Plus they have to wear weird things in their mouth
that look really uncomfortable. Then they think they have
found a stable wormhole that will be a new resource for them,
but then it turns out it is not stable. Luckily they manage
to sell it for awhile first, but soon they will be in the same
situation as before. All they want is to be able to take care
of themselves and be happy but things never get better, which
I can totally understand. Sometimes I daydream about being
hit by a car, and how it might send me into a coma and lots of
years would pass and when I woke up I would have a brand new
life. But I would never do that because being hit by a car
seems like a big risk to take.

Caldonians

Home Planet: Caldonia
Episode: The Price
Rating ***

These aliens are really tall, with only three giant fingers,
and huge heads. Their people are dedicated to being scholars
and scientists, which makes sense because of how big their
heads are. It seems like having a head as big as theirs is
would be a good advantage if you were a scientist.

Acamarians

Home Planet: Acamar III
Episode: The Vengeance Factor
Rating ***

Half of these aliens dress like normal Star Trek aliens, and
the other half dress like people from Mad Max. Most of these
aliens have face tattoos. Sometimes they look okay, but with
the Mad Max ones a lot of the time it looks like they have
moldy cottage cheese on their face. A century ago these aliens
had really violent feuds between different clans. They were so
bad that they threatened to destroy their civilization, so they
stopped doing them. We find out that one of the clans made a
woman who would never age and always stay beautiful and was also poisonous to people in a different clan. It's
weird how no one seems that surprised that this civilization
has the ability to make it so that people don't age. Later
on the woman is about to kill a guy, and Riker tells the guy
to sit still while he repeatedly shoots the woman, even though
the guy who was about to be killed had plenty of time to just
walk away. They could have easily just arrested her, it's
weird that Riker feels the need to phaser her to death instead.

Angosians

Home Planet: Angosia III
Episode The Hunted
Rating ***** for supersoldiers, ** for everyone else

These are aliens who value intelligence and say that they
are nonviolent. But apparently they got into a war somehow, so they genetically engineered some of the people in
their army to turn them into unstoppable supersoldiers.
These guys are like the ultimate badass. They don't give
off life signs, they can resist transporter beams, one of
them fought off five Enterprise people at once, and they
are super cunning and good with military strategy. They
are like the Star Trek version of Aragorn. Pretty much
the only person on the Enterprise who is a match for one
of these guys is Data. Everyone on the Enterprise keeps
falling for this guys tricks over and over except for Data.
Sometimes I think if he wasn't on the ship they would fly
into an asteroid in like five minutes. It is crazy that
Riker outranks Data. Data is better than Riker in pretty
much every way possible. I bet Data could even grow a better beard than Riker is he wanted to. The Angosians claim
to be super smart, but it doesn't stop them from acting like
dicks to their soldiers once the war ended.

Rutians

Home Planet: Rutia IV
Episode The High Ground
Rating ***

These aliens look a lot like humans, except that all the dudes
have weird skunk hairstyles where they have one grey streak
of hair. The main guy of these aliens that we meet kidnaps Dr.
Crusher. Some people call him a terrorist, but the people who
call him a terrorist seem like assholes. He might kill people,
and kidnap Dr. Crusher, but he seems way nicer than the other
side. It reminds me of some of my friends that I have made
this year. One of my teachers told me that I shouldn't hang
out with them because they are a bad influence, but they are
way nicer to me than anyone at my old school was, and one of
them is a really good artist. Mark can draw cartoon characters
like Calvin from Calvin and Hobbes so good that you wouldn't
know that it wasn't the real thing. Plus then we found out
that that teacher made out with one of his students last year.
Just because some kids wear a shirt that has a pot leaf on it
doesn't mean they are bad people, just like the alien in this
episode. Yeah he kidnaps Dr. Crusher, but he does it because he
wants her to cure sick people.

Gomtuu

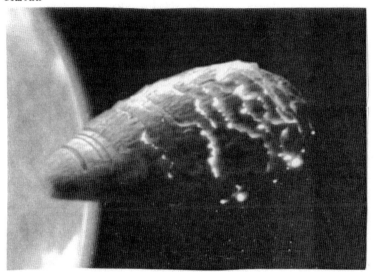

Home Planet: ?
Episode: Tin Man
Rating ***

This is a ship that is also an alien. It looks like a pine
cone, or maybe an almond. Thousands of years ago there was
an explosion in space that killed it's crew, and so it has
wandered around space since then, looking for other aliens
like it. Finally because it is so lonely it decides to sit
next to a star when it goes supernova so it will die. Which
I can understand, there are times I get really depressed
and I think about killing myself. Last winter there was a
few weeks where every night I would get drunk on Lister-
ine and walk to this footbridge that was near the college
by my house. Sometimes I would think about jumping in the
river, but mostly I was just hoping that one of the college
students would wonder why I was there and try to talk to
me. Which is basically what happens in this episode, the
Enterprise comes along and there is a Betazoid guy on board
who is really unhappy, but him and Gomtuu become friends.
Nothing like that ever happened to me though.

Nanites

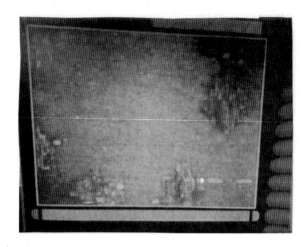

Home Planet: Enterprise
Episode: Evolution
Rating ****

These are tiny robots that are supposed to help out during
surgeries, but Wesley accidentally gives them the power to
evolve, and they start to take over the ship. This episode
is pretty good for making you realize how lame humans are.
Because the nanites go from nothing to being able to talk
in like three days, but it took humans millions of years
to be able to do that. The Enterprise agrees to give them
their own planet so they won't eat the entire ship, but it
seems like once they get an entire planet at the rate they
are growing it will only be like a day before they are
building spaceships, and in a week they will have conquered
the entire galaxy. Star Trek takes place like 400 years
in the future, and after all that time humans still pretty
much seem exactly the same. They never show toilets on the
Enterprise, so maybe humans don't have to go to the bath
room anymore, but that is still not very impressive compared
to the nanites.

Varria

Home Planet: ?
Episode: The Most Toys
Rating **

We never learn the name of the aliens that this woman comes
from. She is a crewmember on Kiva Fajo's ship, and she tries
to help Data escape, but she is killed. There is a disruptor
lying on the floor between her and Fajo, and she tries to dive
for it, but she does a really bad job. I am good at running,
but most things in gym that I am awful at, and even I could
do a better job than she did. She basically just falls on the
ground without jumping for it at all. One of the things I really like about my new school is that there aren't dumb gym
classes like we used to have, they mostly just make us run
laps. The worst thing at my old schools gym class was they
made us do a sit up competition, and they told us to do them
in a certain way, but I was the only one who did. Everyone
else basically cheated, and so the only person I did better
than was the kid who had cerebal palsy. I know I am bad at
sports but that was still BS.

Zilbanian

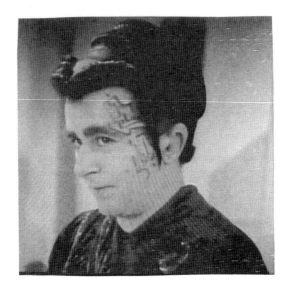

Home Planet: ?
Episode: The Most Toys
Rating ***

I don't know what to think about this guy. On one hand, he
really likes Data. I mean, there are people on the Enterprise
who are friends with Data, but none of them like him enough
to kidnap him. It would be one thing if he was just trying to
ransom Data, but he's not. He wants to hang out with Data.
So obviously he has good taste, unlike the Ferengi who kidnaps
Troi and Riker. But he is a jerk to Data, and kidnapping and
murdering people are both sucky things to do.

Awesome!

Lyaians

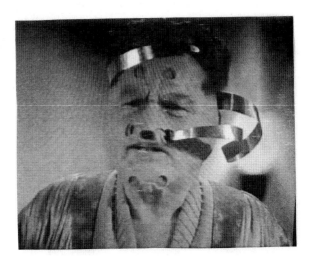

Home Planet: Lya IV
Episode: The Most Toys
Rating **

I think this might be the ugliest alien that has ever been
on Star Trek. You would think that a giant blob alien would
be uglier, but there is something about having extra nostrils
all over your face that looks really nasty. Plus he has some
weird metal thing that wraps around his head going in one
of them. I don't get it at all. It is like at school, some of
the girls have their nose pierced, but I think noses look much
better without piercings in them.

Koinonians

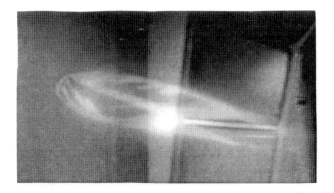

Home Planet: ?
Episode The Bonding
Rating ****

These aliens are blobs of blue energy that fly around, and
they have the ability to basically turn anything into a
holodeck. There was a kid on the Enterprise whose mom died
in an away mission, and these aliens found out about it so
they appeared to him as his dead mom and offered to let him
live with them on the planet in a replica of his house from
Earth. The crew of the Enterprise stops this from happening,
but I think that is some BS. That kid had both his parent
die. He had a sucky life, and if some aliens wanted him to
live in paradise with him he should have gotten to make that
choice. There is another episode from this season with a guy
named Barcalay, and it was great. He is really nervous and
anxious, and everyone makes fun of him, and then tells him
he has nothing to be afraid of, but they don't know that
they're talking about. They all have friends and are popular and have no problems. They don't know what it's like to
be scared or to have a shitty life and dead parents. People
on the Enterprise need to mind their own business sometimes
and stop acting like they have any idea how hard things are
for other people.

Legarans

Home Planet: Legara IV
Episode: Sarek
Rating **

We don't ever get to see these aliens, or even any of their
ships. Just their slime. They are coming aboard the Enterprise to sign a treaty, but I don't see why the Federation
is even bothering. It took the Legarans 93 years to agree
to sign the treaty because they have such a big tools, plus
they are really demanding about there being no furniture in
the room they are staying in, plus they like to hang out in
a tub of smelly goo that is 150 degrees Celsius. They sound
like assholes. The Federation has gotten along fine without
them, and it's not like they are gonna make a treaty with
the Klingons. It seems like a waste of time to be friends
with an alien like this.

Bre'elians

Home Planet: Bre'el IV
Episode Deja Q
Rating *

I don't know why, but these aliens seem like Asian people
to me. They complain a lot and lay guilt trips on the Enterprise, but that's not why they seem Asian. A moon is
about to crash into their planet, and the Enterprise shows
up to stop it from happening. And it seems like all they do
is complain, like the Enterprise isn't trying hard enough,
or to talk about how many people will die if the Enterprise
screws up, even though they aren't doing anything at all. I
think it is complete BS when people act like this, and I am
sick of it. It's not my fault that my mom is a fucking loser
and never does anything, so she should stop getting mad at
me like it is. There are so many things I hate about my
life. I can't wait until I am 18 and I don't have to deal
with this shit anymore.

Calamarains

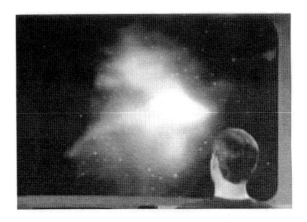

Home Planet: ?
Episode Deja Q
Rating **

These aliens are giant balls of gas, which is lame. I am
okay with there being all sorts of weird looking organic
aliens, and energy aliens seem fine, but gas aliens is a
little bit dumb. In the episode they are able to attack the
Enterprise somehow, but this seems like cheating on the part
of the writers. There is nothing scary about an alien made
out of gas.

Tanugans

Home Planet: Tanuga IV
Episode: A Matter of Perspective
Rating *

There is nothing about these aliens that doesn't make them
assholes. They rip off the Federation so they can make
weapons for other aliens, they try to murder Riker, they
cheat on their husbands, and they give inaccurate testimony
during depositions.

Chalnoth

Home Planet: Chalna
Episode Allegiance
Rating ***

These are giant, hairy, warlike aliens. They are violent
anarchists, which is weird. Not because they are anarchists,
that is fine. When I was in middle school we would have social studies classes where they would teach us BS about the
government, but now that I am older I realize that both the
Democrats and Republicans are liars, so being an anarchist
seems pretty cool. The weird thing about them is I don't
understand how they managed to build things like spaceships
if they have no government and don't seem to like to do
anything but threaten and stab people.

Kidnapper Aliens

Home Planet: ?
Episode: Allegienace
Rating **

These are aliens who kidnap Picard and lock him in a room with
some other aliens, and also they send a doppleganger to take
Picard's place on the Enterprise. These aliens say that they
communicate psychicly, and they are all identical, and they did
these things to better understand behavior and concepts like
authority. But apparently they have already kidnapped some
other aliens to discover seduction techniques, because the fake
Picard totally puts the moves on Dr. Crusher, and then he sings
suspiciously. Other things about these aliens are that they
have giant heads with crazy nostrils, and that they wear very
tight pants that makes their butts stand out.

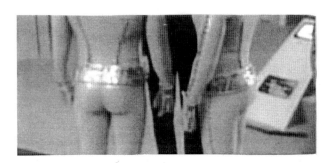

Bolians

Home Planet: Bolarus IX
Episode: Allegiance
Rating ?

I don't even know if I should include this alien, because we
only meet one, and they are an impostor. So I might be giving you incorrect information. The one we meet often seems
sort of nervous, but maybe these aren't usually nervous
aliens, maybe she was nervous because she was actually three
other aliens pretending to be a Bolian, and they were worried they would get caught. I don't see why it took three
of these aliens to impersonate her, especially since it only
took one alien to impersonate Picard. Maybe it is really
tricky for them to do hair? Irregardless, these are blue
aliens that have a line running down the middle of their
head, so if you see one you will at least know what they are
supposed to look like.

Mizarians

Home Planet: Mizar II
Episode Allegiance
Rating ***

These aliens are supposed to be really smart, but the one we
meet is kind of stuck up about it too. They consider themselves to be very peaceful and to not have any enemies, but
other aliens seem to think that these guys are just cowards who
don't put up any resistance when they get invaded. Earlier
this year I got mugged on my way to school and someone tried
to steal the walkman I had just got for my birthday. I begged
the guy not to take and I promised him I would leave money for
him at the bus stop the next day, but then I just started taking a different bus to school. When I told my teachers about
it they said I was very smart not to try and fight him, that a
Walkman is not worth getting injured over. But I don't think
being smart had anything to do with it. I was way to scared
to even think about fighting that guy. He was wearing a big
puffy jacket, and some of the kids at school said that people
wear jackets like that so that they can hide sawed off shotguns
underneath them. The Mizarians brag about how peaceful they
are, but it is way easier to do the "smart" thing. I think they
were just cowards taking the easy way out and they are too
conceited to admit it.

Vorgon

Home Planet: ?
Episode Captain's Holiday
Rating ***

These aliens are time travellers from the 27th century. They
tried to steal a powerful weapon in the future, so the in-
ventor hid the weapon in the 22nd century, and then Picard
found it in the 24th century, so they visit him to try to get
it back. But then Picard finds out that they are thieves
so he destroys it. Which doesn't make a lot of sense to me,
once they find out where it is they should just travel back
in time and look in the hiding spot. This is a pretty good
episode, but it doesn't do a very good job with time travel.
I read a book this year about time travel called Slaughterhouse Five. It does a great job with time travel, and it is
probably the best book I have ever read, even better than
Lord of the Rings. I can't believe they wasted my time in
middle school reading BS like Jacob Have I Loved when I
could have been reading Slaughterhouse Five. Anyways, the
important things about these aliens is that they are thieves,
and they have pointy heads, and that they can travel
through time by touching the side of their head. Also, you
should make sure not to get them confused with Vogons, which
are aliens in Hitchhikers Guide to the Galaxy, which is another good book to read.

Risians

Home Planet: Risa
Episode: Captain's Holiday
Rating: **

These aliens look like humans except that they have a sticker
on their forehead. They run a vacation planet. I don't really care for these aliens. They remind me a lot of the Edo
aliens from the first season, because it seems like all they care
about is partying and having sex. All the kids I have known at
school like that are the beautiful popular kids, and they are
always douchebags. I think probably the more an alien cares
about having fun the less interesting they are. That is why
Data and the Borg and the Vulcans are the coolest aliens on
Star Trek. The one thing the Risians do that I think is a good
idea is that they have statues that you can carry around with
you that lets people know that you are interested in making out. Picard has one sitting next to him when he is reading
and five women try to put the moves on him. I know I am not
very good at talking to girls at school, and I think if there
was something like this in the real world it would make things
a lot less complicated.

Algolians

Home Planet: Algol
Episodes: Menage a Troi
Rating: **

This alien stands around at the back of a party playing an unnecessarily complicated chime xylophone thing. It
is like six feet long but they just play four notes over and
over for the whole party. They are a pretty lame alien, but
that makes sense because this is an episode with Troi's mom,
and those are always the worst. Sometimes I think it makes
sense that Troi is the worst person on the Enterprise because
her mom is so annoying, but then I think about how my mom
is a bitch and I am not like that, so that is no excuse. All
my mom does is lay around and watch tv and talk shit about
people. She is always getting mad at me for BS reasons just
because she is unhappy. If I had Deanna's mom and I was
psychic, there is no way I would turn out as lame as her.

Zalkonians

Home Planet: Zalkon
Episode: Transifigurations
Rating ***

These are aliens with telekinetic powers who are about
to evolve. Also their faces look like they are melting. One of
them is really nice, and has magical healing powers that get
stronger and stronger until he turns into the glowing light
bulb man. But it seems like most of these aliens are jerks.
Everyone in the Federation is scared of the Borg, and the Borg
are really powerful, and the two part episode with the Borg is
definitely the best episodes of tv ever. But these aliens actually seem like they are scarier than the Borg. Because the
Borg still need to shoot at the Enterprise, and get through the
shields. But the captain on the Zalkonian ship just uses the
Force and everyone on the Enterprise starts choking to death.

I think it is lame that these aliens are about to evolve.
You would think that if a race of aliens would evolve, it
would be a cool one like the Vulcans, and not some aliens that
murder all the members of their species that start showing
signs of being different. Star Trek is supposed to be a show
about how much better things will get, but this episode is
proof that there is still dumb BS in the future where jerks get
things they don't deserve.

SEASON FOUR

FIRST PUBLISHED: 1993
AUTHOR AGE: 14

A Field Guide
to the Aliens of

STAR TREK
THE NEXT GENERATION

Season Four

a zine by Joshua Chapman

Introduction

This is my fourth zine about the aliens of Star Trek.
I wrote the first two for my school, and the third
one I mostly just gave out to my friends at school,
but I don't think I will do that anymore because I
don't want to risk any of the adults in the school
reading this. I don't know what I will do with these
yet, but I like thinking about Star Trek so I will
probably keep making them. If you are reading this
and you haven't seen any of the other issues the
main things you should know is that Data and the
Vulcans are the best aliens, and Counsellor Troi and
her mom are the worst.

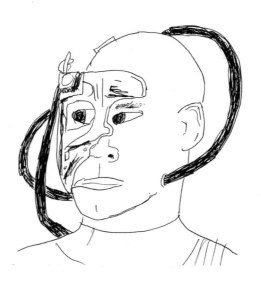

Talarian

Home Planet: ?
Episode: Suddenly Human
Rating: **

These aliens are sexist and warlike, and even though they are
constantly talking about how strong they are, when they are
worried they make this really annoying whining noise like
they are a bunch of stupid diaper babies. The only good
thing about these aliens is that they are considered to be an
adult when they are 14. There is one human who was kidnapped by some of these aliens when he was a baby, and when
he was old enough he was given the choice of staying with
the Talarians or living with the Federation. It is awesome
that they let him choose. Last year in gym class normally I
always wore sweatpants but one day they made me wear shorts
and they found out that I was cutting my legs. After they
found out the counselor talked to me and said they would see
about maybe arranging it so that I didn't have to stay with
my mom anymore but in the end they didn't do shit. Afterwards the counselor tried telling me that I shouldn't cut
myself but fuck him. If he had to live with my mom I bet
he would cut himself too. These guys might be assholes but at
least they don't jerk their kids around.

Barash

Home Planet : Alpha Onias III
Episode: Future Imperfect
Rating *

This is probably the most stereotypical looking alien
that has ever been on Star Trek. Most of the aliens usually look like people, but this one just looks like the
way you would expect a normal alien to look. Barash was
abandoned on his planet by his parents. They gave him
something like a holodeck to keep him company, except
that it's a cave. But eventually he gets lonely and when
Riker crashes on the planet Barash kidnaps him and tries
to force him into loving him, which is a really fucked up
thing to do. I don't care how lonely you are, if you try
to guilt or blackmail someone into caring for you then
you are an asshole.

Gamelanians

Home Planet: Gamelan V
Episode: Final Mission
Rating: **

The two big deals about these aliens is that they are
really crazy looking, and they seem incompetent. There
are like twenty ugly things going on with their faces
but the weirdest thing is that they have strands of
skin stretching vertically across their mouth. This
seems like it would make eating very inconvenient, and
that they basically would just have to drink everything
through a straw. They send the Enterprise a distress
signal because an old space barge with radioactive stuff
on it has drifted close to their planet and they don't
know how to deal with it. I am suspicious of this. If
their entire planet is unable to defend itself from an
abandoned space barge I don't see how they could possi-
bly not have been invaded by now.

Pentarusian

Home Planet: Pentarus V
Episode: Final Mission
Rating: ***

It seems like a lot of these aliens are supposed to be min-
ers. They basically look human except for bumpier foreheads,
which is true of a lot of aliens for this season. We only meet
one of these guys, a man named Dirgo who captains a crappy
mining shuttle. He has a big chip on his shoulder about how
he doesn't have fancy Federation ships. He talks like his
shuttle is still really good, even though it basically falls
apart as soon as they get into space. Then they crash on a
planet and he tries to hide alcohol from Picard and Wesley
because he is probably an alcoholic. Which is understandable
because it seems like he has a shitty life. I know I shouldn't
drink because of what happened to my dad but for a little
bit I tried drinking because it made me not care as much when
my mom was acting crazy. But in the end it just made things
worse because when she found out I was drinking she just
started screaming and hitting herself and breaking dishes and
crying about being a bad parent. Which is why now I just do
cutting. It is much easier to hide from her and it is better
to have her laying on the couch all day watching soap operas
than it is to have to listen to her screaming and slamming
doors.

Two Dimensional Beings

Home Planet: ?
Episode: The Loss
Rating: ****

These things are great because they show how awful Troi is.
The Enterprise gets caught in a giant field of these and because there are so many of them they shut off Troi's psychic
powers. When this happens she completely freaks out and
basically acts like my mom does all the time. She is like
a fucking child and mean and petty and whenever anyone
tries to comfort her she acts like they are an asshole even
though the person is just trying to help. Fuck her. She is
such a fucking bitch. Most of the time it is like she won't
be happy until she has destroyed everything good in my
life. Like if I am not constantly as miserable as her it is
an insult to her. They are both so fucking selfish and act
like nothing in the world matters besides their own feelings.
Last time I tried to go to my friend Mike's house she locked
herself in the bathroom with her gun to force me to stay
and prove that I loved her which is so fucking bullshit. I
hate that she does that to me and there are so many times
that I think about that and get so angry that I start shaking. I wish the Enterprise would have stayed stuck in the
two dimensional creatures. Troi doesn't deserve to have a
happy ending.

Cardassians

Home Planet: Cardassia Prime
Episode: The Wounded
Rating: ****

These aliens seem pretty sneaky, but overall they basically act
like humans. It's not like how the Klingons are always super
aggressive or the Ferengi are really greedy or the Betazoids are
annoying losers. The Cardassians seem to have several different emotions, which is pretty rare for aliens. The Federation
used to be at war with the Cardassians and because of it a lot
of Federation people are racist against Cardassians. In this
episode O'Brien talks about how when he was fighting in the
war he accidentally killed a Cardassian, and he had to become
tough to deal with the guilt, and he hated the Cardassians for
that, and he hates himself for hating the Cardassians. Emotions are fucked. The counsellors at school used to tell me that
I shouldn't want to be like Data or the Vulcans, that emotions
are good things, but I have never seen any evidence that proves
me wrong.

Ventaxians

Home Planet: Ventax II
Episode: Devil's Due
Rating **

These are some human looking aliens that have a peaceful,
agrarian society. A thousand years ago they claim they made
a deal with the devil to have a nice planet, but it seems
like they should also have wished to not be giant chumps.
Because in the present a con artist shows up claming to be
the devil and they totally fall for it, even though nothing she does is that impressive. You would think that in the
future maybe people would have learned to be less gullible,
but I guess not.

Ardra

Home Planet: ?
Episode: Devil's Due
Rating ***

Ardra is the name of an alien who tries to trick the Ventaxians into thinking she is the devil, so they will make
her ruler of their planet. At first it seems like she has
the ability to shapeshift, but she is just doing it with the
the transporter and holograms. She turns into the Klingon
devil, and then the human devil. This freaks people out, and
I don't know why the Federation doesn't do this more often.
It seems like really useful technology. If the Enterprise
had people on an away mission and someone attacked them, you
could just use the transporters to make it look like everyone
turned into dinosaurs. Or invisible. Either way it would
definitely give them a big advantage. The thing I really
don't understand is why Ardra even wants to be ruler of the
Ventaxians. It seems like it would not be all that great to
be worshiped by people who are so stupid you can trick them
into thinking you're the devil.

Paxans

Home Planet: ?
Episode: Clues
Rating ***

These are some energy aliens that look like green clouds
of gas. They are super xenophobic and hate all other life
forms. When an alien comes into their system they knock
them unconscious and wipe their memory and make them
think they went through a wormhole. At one point the
Paxans take control of Troi's body, and then Worf tries to
attack her but she breaks his wrist then throws him across
the room, which doesn't make any sense. It's not like when
they take over her body they made her grow new muscles.
I don't understand why she would suddenly have super
strength. Anyways, their plan doesn't work because Data is
immune to their attack, and then he has to try and trick
the Enterprise into not going back to the Paxan planet. It
doesn't work, but that has more to do with Picard giving
Data bad orders. Earlier in this season Data takes over
the Enterprise without even breaking a sweat, and that was
awesome. I am sure if it was all up to him Data could have
definitely found a way to make sure the Enterprise didn't
go back.

Malcorians

Home Planet: Malcor III
Episode First Contact
Rating ***

These aliens are humanoid looking, except that they have
bumpier foreheads, and it looks like they are wearing weird
flesh mittens on their hands. In a lot of ways they seem
like they are like modern humans. Their technology doesn't
seem like it is too much more advanced than ours, except
that they are about to discover warp drives. They are also
like us in that there are a few cool people on their planet,
but also lots of jerks. One of the cool people is a scientist
named Mirasta. She is the first person Picard talks to when
he makes first contact. She wants the Malcorians to join the
Federation, but the President says no because there are too
many conservative assholes in their society. At the end of
the episode she asks if she can stay on the Enterprise and
Picard says yes. The first time I saw this episode I cried at
the end because I have wanted that for so long and it made
me happy to see it happen for someone. I know if people
at school read this they will probably make fun of me but
I don't give a fuck what they think anymore. They don't
know what my life is like. All I have wanted for years is
live on the Enterprise. I have thought about this and I
could probably even get a job being a historian for them
and answer any questions they had about the past.

Space Fish

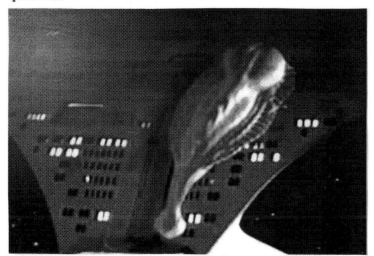

Home Planet: ?
Episode: Galaxy's Child
Rating ***

This is an alien that lives in outer space. The Enterprise accidentally kills one of these because it attacked the Enterprise
because it was pregnant. These aliens basically look like one
of those kinds of fish that sticks to the side of the tank in an
aquarium. It is weird to me that every time on Star Trek that
they encounter an alien that lives in outer space, it always
looks like a sucker fish, or a jellyfish, or a snowflake, instead
of a normal looking thing. Since these creatures are flying
around in space, you would think there would be more space
birds or something like that. Space cats would be the best in
my opinion, but that is probably not realistic.

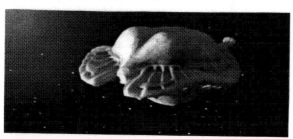

Tarchannians

Home Planet: Tarchannen III
Episode: Identity Crisis
Rating **

The aliens on this planet have an unusual way of reproducing. When a human or somebody comes to their planet, these aliens sneak up to them and infect them with a parasite that will transform them into a Tarchannian alien. This seems like an incredibly stupid way to reproduce. For one thing, it is probably way nicer just to have sex. Also, they need to have aliens constantly coming to their planet in order to transform them. I guess it has worked okay for them so far, but it seems very inefficient. Once someone gets infected, nothing happens for like five years, then the person freaks out and steals a shuttlecraft and flies to this planet, and by the end it is like they are a completely new creature. I think a lot about what it would be like to wake up with a new life. I have decided that I don't want to kill myself, but sometimes I daydream that maybe I could be hit by a car or something and I would fall into a coma for like ten years and when I woke up my life would be completely different because everyone I know now would be gone. It would be awesome to wake up as a new alien, but I am not sure I would want to be one of these aliens because of how ugly they are. I guess that is why they developed invisibility powers, because they didn't want other people to see how dumb they look covered in their stupid blue veins.

Cytherians

Home Planet: ?
Episode: The Nth Degree
Rating ****

These aliens are giant floating space heads that live in the
center of the galaxy. They want to learn more about the universe but they don't want to leave the their planet so they
just hijack other aliens and force them to come visit them.
This seems a little strange to me, but it is also basically the
same thing as home schooling and in my experience people who
have been home schooled are sort of like this. There was one
girl in my school who used to be home schooled. I liked her,
and once she even invited me over to her house to smoke pot
with her. But then I found out that she had a big crush on my
friend Mike and I saw inside her locker and it was filled with
scraps of paper and pens and used tissues and stuff. She had
been collecting every item that Mike had touched and thrown
away for several weeks. After I found out about that I wasn't
really interested in her anymore. This is pretty much the same
as the Cytherians, they seem really out of touch with how to
not act weird, which is why I think it's a home schooling thing.

Kaelon

Home Planet: Kaelon II
Episode: Half a Life
Rating ***

These are some human looking aliens except that they have hideous black veins on their foreheads. All of these aliens seem too polite. We see one of these aliens who is a scientist and he falls in love with Troi's mom after like two days, but mostly just because apparently women on his planet don't know how to flirt and he is flabbergasted that there is a lady who will drop hints about wanting to make out with him. He is trying to stop his planets sun from exploding, but these aliens all kill themselves when they turn sixty. When Troi's mom finds out about this she guilts him into not killing himself, but then the people on his planet say that they will exile him, and his daughter guilts him into killing himself again. It is a fucked up situation for the guy and I feel really sorry for him. This is another case of people in the Federation thinking they know whats best for everyone. If the scientist wants to kill himself they should not give him a hard time. It is like how the school counsellor told me to talk to him if I am going to cut myself, but I know he will probably tell my mom and I can't have that happen. There are lots of times I wish I could talk to people, but I can't, because if my mom ever found it things would get so much worse. But cutting helps. I don't understand why the counsellor doesn't see that. I cut words into my legs and it is like whispering someone a secret and I don't have to worry about my mom ever finding out. People should be allowed to do what is best for them, just like the scientist should be able to kill himself if he wants to.

Peliar Zel Aliens

Home Planet: Peliar Zel
Episode: The Host
Rating: **

These are some aliens with grey skin and extra nostrils and
forehead ridges. The thing that is unclear is what the top of
their heads look like. All these aliens wear weird hats, but I
don't know if the hats are empty, or if maybe they are form
fitting and that is just what their heads are shaped like.
The Enterprise shows up to deliver an ambassador because two
of this planets moons are about to start fighting. One of the
moons is using an energy source that will destroy the second
moon. I am not really sure why they need an ambassador to
decide this, since killing all the people on the second moon
seems pretty obviously like a thing you shouldn't do.

Trill

Home Planet: Trill
Episodes: The Host
Rating: **

These aliens are disgusting looking slugs that live in
people's stomachs and take over their brains. Dr. Crusher
falls in love with one of these guys, but then the body he
was in is injured, so the slug had to be moved to Riker for
a little bit, and then to some lady. And the lady seemed
perfectly fine with it, which is crazy because when one of
the Trill slugs goes into a new body they basically murder
the person whose body they take over. The host body loses
their consciousness and the slug just hangs out there until
the new body dies, however long that takes. It would be
one thing if they were putting the Trill into babies, but
they're not. I would not want to sacrifice my life just so
some space slug could have more chances to make out with
Dr. Crusher.

SEASON
FIVE

FIRST PUBLISHED: 1994
AUTHOR AGE: 15

A Field Guide
to the Aliens of

Season Five

a zine by Joshua Chapman

Introduction

I don't want to write an introduction for this issue.
It's not like I am getting graded on this shit anymore.
Here is a picture of Data and his cat instead.

Devidians

Home Planet: Devidia II
Episodes: Time's Arrow
Rating: **

These are aliens that live slightly out of phase with us and
are therefore impossible for us to interact with, although
I am not sure what exactly that means. Geordi talks like
they are slightly in the future, and that is why they can't
see them, but I am not sure why they wouldn't still be able
to see the alien at that point in the past. These aliens can
change their shape: sometimes they look like weird glowing
humanoids with giant heads, and sometimes they look like
fancy historical people. They eat human souls or something,
and in order to collect them they go to points in history
where lots of people are dying anyways from plagues so they
can steal the souls without being noticed using a magical
purse. Which is kind of a neat plan, but it seems inefficient. If I was them I would just bust into a daycare and
kill the babies to steal their souls. It's not like they are
going to be able to fight back: they're babies.

The Beast of El Adrel

Home Planet: El Adrel IV
Episode: Darmok
Rating: ****

This alien reminds me a lot of the creature from the movie
Predator, partly because it sort of looks like the Predator, and partly because it can turn itself invisible like
the predator, and partly because it actually is a predator.
These aliens have like the perfect defense mechanism: anyone
who touches them gets an electric shock. This is a really
elegant solution because it means nothing can ever get close
to you. When I was little my mom used to be nice to me, but
if that had never happened then I wouldn't hate it so much
now when she acts like a psychotic bitch all the time. That
is why this alien's defense is so good, because if people
can't get close to you then they can't hurt you.

Children of Tama

Home Planet : ?
Episode: Darmok
Rating ****

This is a super ugly kind of alien. They look like burn
victims, and they have a weird language. People on the
Enterprise say that these aliens only speak in metaphor,
but I studied metaphors in English class and these aliens
use allegory, not metaphor. I am not sure why the people
on the Enterprise wouldn't know that, since they make 10
year old kids take calculus. The captain of these aliens
knows that the Federation can't understand them, so he
kidnaps Picard and makes them fight a third alien so
that teamwork will help Picard understand. He does this
even though he knows the alien is super dangerous, and
it eventually kills him. He sacrifices himself in the
hopes that it will allow peace with the Federation, which
as far as sacrifices go is a pretty noble thing to do. I
think it would be nice to have something in your life
that you believed in enough to want to die for it.

Bajoran

Home Planet: Bajor
Episode: Ensign Ro
Rating: ****

Bajorans were aliens that had built impressive cities tens of
thousands of years ago. Everyone talks about how advanced
they were, but it seems to me like if they were really that
smart it would not have taken them so long to develop space
flight. Then like fifty years ago the Cardassians invaded
Bajor and enslaved the people and basically holocausted
them. One Bajoran named Ro Laren joined up with the Federation and she seems pretty badass, I like her character a
lot. One time she talks about how some Cardassians tricked
her into watching her father being tortured to death, and
how he begged for mercy, and how that disgusted her. It
reminds me of this play we had to read this year in school
called The Crucible. It is about the Salem witch trials.
There is a guy in the play who is a farmer who is accused of
being a wizard, but he thinks the trials are bullshit and he
refuses to say whether he is a wizard. So the people start
piling heavy rocks on him and every time they put another

one on they ask him if he is a wizard, and he just keeps
saying more weight, until he is crushed to death. That guy
is basically my new hero. There are a lot of times at home
when I am dealing with my moms bullshit and she will be
screaming at me about how useless I am and that I have
never loved her and I feel like I am going to explode. It
is like there is an unbearable weight pushing down on me.
I can't think or breathe and there is nothing in me but
hatred of this fucking shit she puts me through when all I
want is for her to be nice like she used to be. I feel like
I can't bear it but then I think of the guy in the play
and how strong he was that he basically died saying fuck
you to those people. That he was saying more weight and
fuck you in the same words. That is what I want. I don't
understand why she is doing this to me, if she is punishing
me for something or what. But when I die I want my last
words to her to be fuck you, so she knows that she failed.

Ktarian

Home Planet: Ktaris
Episode: The Game
Rating: **

These are aliens that look like they have a butt on their
forehead. They make the most addictive video game in the
universe and they use it to brainwash people because they
want to try to take over the Federation. The thing I don't
understand is that their video game looks awful. You
would think that in 400 years they would have learned to
make really good video games, especially since they have
the holodeck. But some game where you have to get a disc
to go into a tube isn't even on the level of an Atari game,
let alone a new game like Doom. Maybe it is like how in
the future they are too dumb to listen to any music besides really old classical music or jazz, instead of really
good music like Nine Inch Nails. Pretty Hate Machine and
Broken were both really good albums, but I think Downward
Spiral is probably the best album of all time. It has only
been out for like a month and I have already listened to
it hundreds of times. I even pretended to be sick the day
after I got it and I listened to it nonstop for 28 hours.

Amarie

Home Planet: ?
Episode: Unification II
Rating ***

This alien works in a bar. She is sort of freaky looking,
since there is no front to her nose, and she has weird things
sticking out of her head. Also, she has four arms, which is
probably why she decided to become a piano player. I think
it would be pretty useful to have four arms, because then
I if I broke one of my arms I would still be able to play
video games with the other three. Sometimes I practice playing video games with my feet in case I do break one of my
arms, that way I won't have as much of a learning curve,
but it hasn't come in useful yet.

Ja'Dar

Home Planet: ?
Episode: New Ground
Rating: **

This is an ugly alien whose chin looks like a melted turtle shell. Based on the information from this episode these are aliens who make bad science decisions, because they are trying to invent warp wave technology which seems like an incredibly dumb idea. They want to get rid of warp drives and just have ships ride waves of warp energy, which is a great as long as you don't mind not being able to stop, or change directions, or control your movements in any way whatsoever.

Ullian

Home Planet: Ull
Episode: Violations
Rating: **

The first thing about these aliens is that they have incredibly ugly ears. The second thing about these aliens
is that they have telepathic powers that they can use to
help people retrieve lost memories, but also to mind rape
people. When we meet them, it is some parents and their
son, and the father is a complete asshole to the son and he
constantly mocks and embarasses him. Then some people get
mind raped and they think it is the father, but it actually
turns out to be the son, which should have been incredibly
obvious since he spends the entire episode looking at people
suspiciously. I don't think the son should have mind raped
those people but I think the father deserved everything he
got. It is his fault for being an asshole. It is his fault
for turning his son into a monster. I do not blame the son
at all for trying to frame his father.

Satarran

Home Planet: Sothis III
Episode: Conundrum
Rating **

These aliens are strange. Even though they have sort of
crappy military technology, they still manage to instantly
incapacitate everyone on the Enterprise, then wipe their
memories, then alter the records on the Enterprise. I would
think that the Federation would have some sort of security
system in place so that other aliens can't tamper with the
computer, but I guess not. The reason they do all this is
because they are at war with another group of aliens with
lame weapons, and they are too chickenshit to kill those
aliens themselves, so they try to trick the Enterprise into
doing it for them. Even though these aliens are pretty
sneaky, I have no respect for them. If you are going to
hurt someone, you should not play games or make someone
else do your dirty work. That shit is for children. I read
a book this year called Brave New World that was really
good. It was about how people need to stop acting like
babies all the time. I should like these aliens: they are
clever and they look like ghouls or some other monster from
Dungeons and Dragons, but I have no more patience for this
type of immature BS. People need to act like adults and
start taking responsibility for the shit they do.

Lysians

Home Planet: ?
Episode: Conundrum
Rating ***

We don't really know much about the Lysians except that
they are in a war against the Satarrans, and they have
crappy technology. There is not much to say about them
so instead I am gonna talk about how what utter bullshit
it is that the writers would have Troi beat Data at chess.
Troi is awful. She is not smart and she is not funny. She
is just weak and whiny and useless. Data has the knowledge
of all the greatest chess masters in history in his brain.
He fought the galaxy's greatest master of Stratagema to
a standstill. He has no emotions for Troi to read. It is
completely ridiculous that Troi would be able to last more
than five moves against Data, let alone beat him. Data is
basically perfect. Data is my goal. I don't want emotions
anymore. I don't want to feel. That is the only way I will
ever survive this. She doesn't want to change. She tells
the social workers she does, but if she wanted to change she
wouldn't keep doing this to me. She says she is sorry but
if she meant it she would stop. They tell me to smile at
her apologies and to say I forgive her but I just want to
spit acid in her fucking face.

Ux-Malians

Home Planet: Mab-Bu VI
Episode Power Play
Rating **

These aliens used to have bodies, but now they are just
some energy balls. They were criminals who had their
bodies taken from them, and they were exiled to a shitty
planet. Then the Enterprise shows up and three of them
possess Troi, Data and O'Brien. Once they are possessed
they are incredibly cruel and cold and emotionless. They
take some hostages in Ten Forward and Keiko is there and
the way that O'Brien treats her it is like he is empty of
everything he used to be. I feel like this sometimes and
it is really scary. My mom will start with her stupid
childish needy bullshit and I will get so angry it is like
something else takes control of me and I just want to hurt
something. A few weeks ago when this happened my cat came
near me and I don't know what happened but I kicked it
so hard and it was frightened of me for days afterwards
and now I am scared to go near it because I am worried it
might happen again. I love my cat so much and I fucking
hate her that she made me hurt it. I just want to lay in
my bed and have my cat lick my hair until I feel better
like I used to but I think I am empty now. I think there
is nothing good left in me to bring back.

J'Naii

Home Planet: J'naii
Episode: The Outcast
Rating **

These are some aliens that claim to be androgynous even
though they are clearly all female. They talk a lot about
how their society has evolved beyond gender, but they are
sort of snotty about it. I would think that a better prior-
ity would be for them to evolve out of being self righteous
assholes before they worry about the gender stuff. Riker
starts flirting with one of these aliens because he is sort
of a perv who can't help flirting with every alien he meets,
and it turns out this alien thinks she is female even though
that is against the law in their society. Then Riker makes
out with her which is a really fucked up thing for him to
do. It's not like anything bad will happen to him if the
Federation finds out, but when the J'naii find out that
this alien likes to be female they brainwash her. Riker was
careless with her. He did whatever he wanted just like he
always does. She trusted him and now this woman who has
known nothing but shame and sadness and hating herself has
had her life somehow get even worse. At least before she at
least had her anger over how fucked up her situation was,
but they took that away from her too.

Kostolainians

Home Planet: Kostolain
Episode: Cost of Living
Rating **

This is without a doubt the worst possible episode of Star
Trek. Every moment of it makes me mad. Not only is Troi in
it a lot, and also her mom, and also Alexander who is really annoying, but on the holodeck they also create some
bullshit pleasure colony which is filled with fucking
sucky ass shit. It is like some stupid bubble mime alien
who makes annoying faces and some fake Dr Seuss arguing
aliens and a dumbass alien who juggles three balls. Who
the fuck cares about juggling three balls? There are kids
in my school who can do that right now. If you live in
the future and in space then juggling three fucking balls
does not cut it. But the main aliens of this episode are
some stuck up old guys who love rules and protocol. And
normally they would seem like assholes but in this episode
they seem like the greatest aliens in the world because they
have to deal with so much bullshit that I don't blame them
at all for getting pissed off because people don't follow
timetables.

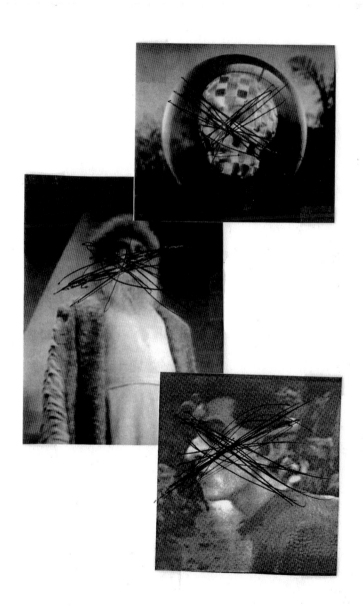

Kriosian

Home Planet: Krios Prime
Episode: The Perfect Mate
Rating ***

These aliens look just like the Valtese. Once every hundred
years with these aliens a woman is born who has psychic
powers and she uses them to turn herself into the ultimate mate for whoever she decides to be with. Also she has
to live inside a giant egg for awhile, which is weird. She
reads mens minds to figure out stuff about them, plus she
secretes chemicals to make men fall in love with her. It is
basically like she just casts a love spell on all the men
she meets. I have some friends at school who are really into
witchcraft, and they let me borrow some of their books once,
and the stuff this lady does reminds me of the love spells
that were in those books. It's hard for me to take stuff
like that seriously, but it would be awesome if it was true.
I have been reading about magic and wizards since I was
a little kid. I think it would be incredible to have that
kind of power. I am sick of my life. I am sick of always
feeling so helpless. But to be able to do magic, to use it to
be able to cast actual spells and change your life and control people, I can understand why my friends are into it.

Valtese

Home Planet: Valt Minor
Episode: The Perfect Mate
Rating ***

These are aliens who have been at war with another group
of aliens, named the Kriosians, for hundreds of years. Originally they were one race, but then two brothers started
fighting over a girl, and one of the brothers was the leader
of the Valtese, and the other one got the girl and took off
and started his own planet of aliens. Which is moronic shit
to start a war over. I know it is supposed to be like the
Trojan war, but that happened thousands of years ago when
people were stupid and didn't know how to invent things
like light bulbs or computers. It would make sense that the
Trojans would do something dumb like have a war because of
one woman. But the Valtese aliens had spaceships capable of
interstellar travel. They should at least be smart enough
not to have wars that last for centuries just because some
dude kidnapped some lady.

Isabella

Home Planet: FGC 47
Episode: Imaginary Friend
Rating: *

These aliens are some energy balls, but they can take the
shape of people if they want to, also they can read peoples
minds somehow if they fly into someones head. It seems like
whenever there is an alien made out of energy on this show,
they are always ball shaped. One of them turns into the
imaginary friend of a girl, and she is pretty much the worst
person alive in Star Trek. She is manipulative and mean and
bitchy and vindictive. Everyone on the Enterprise is ready to
forgive her even though she summons a bunch of other energy
balls to murder them, but fuck that. I know what it is like
to have someone treat you this way, and you don't forgive
them. It is so fucking ridiculous how much this alien reminds
me of my mom and that is such bullshit. It is bullshit that
she is basically a child and everyone tells me that I have to
be strong and just put up with how badly she acts so she can
get better. I should not have to be the adult in our family.
At the end of the episode the Enterprise gives these aliens a
gift of free energy. I think the Federation shouldn't try so
hard to be nice to aliens who are obviously assholes.

Kataanian

Home Planet: Kataan
Episodes: The Inner Light
Rating: ***

These are some aliens that died out like a thousand years
ago. The Enterprise comes in contact with one of their
probes and it makes Picard think that he is living out his
life on their planet so that people will remember them. In
his other life he has a wife and two kids and he plays a
flute but not very well. I thought this was a good episode,
but I hate it when on tv shows they show happy families
like Picard and his kids because it is all such bullshit.
It is fake. It makes me want to set fire to myself. I feel
empty inside, like there is just a shell of me what walks
around, and I hate that there is even an image of me that
exists in the same world as fake shit like this. Looking
like a normal person feels like I am supporting this lie of
bullshit happy families.

SEASONS
SIX & SEVEN

FIRST PUBLISHED: 1995
AUTHOR AGE: 16

A Field Guide
to the Aliens of

STAR TREK
THE NEXT GENERATION

Seasons Six and
Seven

a zine by
Joshua Chapman

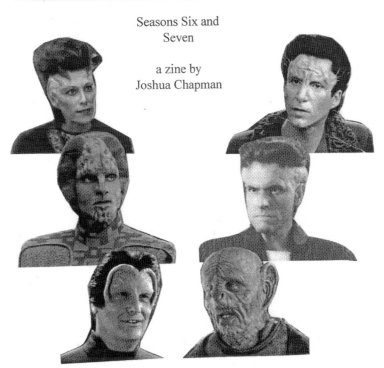

Introduction

This is going to be my last issue. I know that it would make more sense for there to be seven issues since there were seven seasons of the show, but I am going to graduate high school next month, and I don't know what is going to happen after that. I might not get a chance to write any more after this, so I am just going to have this be a double issue.

I don't know what I am going to do after I graduate. I have thought a lot about leaving home once I finish school, because I fucking hate my life here. Part of me wants to get as far away from my mom as possible, but I am worried what will happen if I do. I hate her, and I hate the way she treats me, but I still don't want her to die. She didn't always used to be this way. Things have gotten so much worse the last few years, and I don't know what she would do if I wasn't around anymore. I think she would probably kill herself, or end up being one of those crazy ladies who talks to themselves on the bus. So I am fucking trapped. I don't know what to do. I have been worrying about this for months, and I keep putting off the decision because either way I am fucked, and every day that passes the pressure just gets worse and worse. So I have decided to give myself a deadline: I am going to write a review of one alien a day from now on, and when I am done I will make my decision.

PS Preemptive Strike would have made a much better season finale than All Good Things, because in the actual season finale Q basically just gives Picard the answer to the pardox, which is dumb.

Season Six

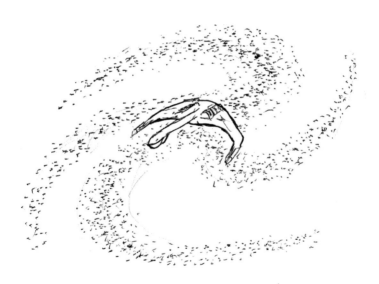

Lumerians

Home Planet: ?
Episode: Man of the People
Rating: *

This dude is an asshole. He doesn't want to have to deal with his negative
emotions, so he tricks women into channeling all his negative thoughts, and
when this happens they act crazy and age super fast. He does this to Troi
and when this happens she is even more insufferable than normal. The weird
thing is, Star Trek is usually a show that is all about science, but what this
dude does is basically just magic. There is a ritual and crystals and everything. I have been studying magic a lot this past year. There is a family
that I babysit for sometimes, and the mom is a Wiccan, and I read some of
her books but I didn't really care for them. They were written by some lady
named Starhawk, which is a hippie name, and the books are more about wor-
shipping some goddess than casting spells. Then when I was at the bookstore
I found a book called the Necronomicon, which at first seemed really cool,
but then I realized that if there were books that had spells that could summon
ancient gods, it probably would be some giant old-looking book with a leather cover, and not a paperback that I bought at Waldenbooks. But also there
is a comic I read called Sandman and sometimes people in it do magic. And
the magic in it seems real. Tongues nailed to walls and circles of pebbles
surrounding a pool of blood and calling the moon. In Sandman it seems like
part of magic is ritual but a bigger part of it is will. If you want something
bad enough, and you know how to want for it in the right way, then maybe
you can change things, and that's what the Lumerian guy does.

Solanogens

Home Planet : Sub Space
Episode: Schisms
Rating **

These are aliens that live deep in sub space. I don't know what that
really means. Maybe it is like being from another dimension? This
episode does not really explain that, or why these aliens look sort of like
a cross between a fish and a lizard, and they have giant weird claws.
They decide they want to check out what it is like in our dimension, and
the way they do that is by abducting people and running experiments on
them. This episode was pretty creepy, which was cool, but definitely the
best part of it was that it had Data reciting poems about his cat. Everyone seemed to think the poem wasn't very good, but I don't understand
that at all. I had to read poems in English class and I don't see how this
poem is any different than the stuff they made me read about urns and
trees and shit. It rhymed perfectly, and it's not like a tree is a better thing
to write a poem about than a cat. I think people just arbitrarily decide
which poems and books are good and which aren't and then they just
make up theories to support their bullshit so that they can seem smart. I
think Data's poetry was really good.

Tagrans

Home Planet: Tagra IV
Episode: True Q
Rating: **

These aliens have way too many ridges on their heads. I definitely believe
evolution is a thing, but I don't think it would make sense to produce an alien
that looks like this. No one needs to have a face that is that bumpy. These
aliens polluted their planet really badly, and the Enterprise is trying to help
them out but then things get fucked up and there is a girl who is like a Q in
training and she helps them out. Except rather than make them not want to
pollute their planet anymore, or giving them some new energy that won't
cause pollution, all she does is clean up some of the pollution for the time being. In some ways it is like the Q people can use magic, but at the same time
they don't use spells or words or rituals, so it is not real magic. They just
snap their fingers like they are a character on Bewitched or something. There
is one time in Sandman where a guy turns into a bear, but he still has the
shadow of a human, and then he chews off his shadow. He does this because
someone is hunting him, and he needs to be a new person to escape. But the
point is that his magic is hard and painful and there is a cost to it. That is
what real magic should be like. Not waving your arms back and forth and
wishing for shit.

Tyrans

Home Planet: Tyrus VIIa
Episode: The Quality of Life
Rating: *

These are some aliens that have bumpy foreheads but they pretty much just act like humans. They are not one of the kinds of aliens who all have the same behaviors, like the are all aggressive, or all greedy.. We really only get to see one of these aliens, or at least one alive one. She is working to build a giant drill in space but in the process she accidentally builds a new kind of robotic life form. She was trying to make her life easier by making a bunch of little levitating robots to be her slaves. She doesn't care about them at all, but then Data points out that they might actually have consciousnesses, and she absolutely refuses to believe that the Exocomps are alive. It basically makes her angry because she is worried about losing control over the things she created and probably also because then she would have to admit what an asshole she is for treating them like slaves. Even though they are alive she cannot stand the idea of not forcing them to do things. They run a test on the Exocomps to see if they are alive, and by accident they think the Exocomps fail the test, and when this happens she is almost cruel in how happy she is. She is gloating and smug and mean to Data because it means she will get to keep using them however she wants. She says the difference between the Exocomps is that Dr Soong created Data to be alive, and she created the Exocomps to be tools, but that is bullshit. Just because she didn't want to create children does not give her the right to treat them like fucking shit. Fuck her.

Exocomps

Home Planet: Tyrus VIIa
Episode: The Quality of Life
Rating: ****

These are weird little robots that are programmed to solve problems, and
after they solve enough of them they basically become sentient. People
act like this is a crazy thing, even though this is exactly what happened
when the nanites got loose, and if it has happened twice on the Enterprise
in three years it seems like it probably happens a lot. At first Data is the
only one to realize that they are alive, and when a giant space drill is about
to explode people want to trick the Exocomps to go on a suicide mission to
save Picard and Geordi, but Data won't let them because it is a fucked up
thing to manipulate someone and ruin their life just for your own benefit.
Afterwards Data tries to apologize to Picard but Picard says that protecting
the Exocomps was the most human decision Data had ever made, which
is a fucking bullshit lie because the humans wanted the Exocomps to die.
The human decision would have been to kill them without even giving it a
second thought because they are so fucking selfish.

Haliian

Home Planet: Halii
Episode: Aquiel
Rating *

This lady is awful. I don't even understand how she got accepted into Starfleet. She is boring and annoying and irrational and the special effects makeup that lets you know she is an alien is just two tiny bumps on her forehead. Geordi falls in love with her, but whatever, Geordi falls in love with computer women all the time. That is basically his thing. Plus she tries to have weird crystal sex with him which is obviously a horrible idea because we JUST SAW the weird Lumerian dude cast spells this way like ten episodes ago. People think she might have killed someone, and she says she can't remember what happened, and Geordi tries to help her out but then she destroys evidence. And it's like, how fucking stupid and selfish are you? Geordi is trying to help you and you aren't even taking care of yourself and now you are going to drag him down into your shitty mess too. Stop acting like you are the only one affected by your decisions. Stop fucking doing shit like yours is the only life that you are ruining.

Corvallen

Home Planet: ?
Episode: Face of the Enemy
Rating ***

These aliens look like weird rock creatures. I don't even see how they are alive if their faces are made of rocks, and we don't really get to find out because a Romulan guy kills them like five seconds after they show up. They seem more like something you would find in the Monsters Manual than on Star Trek. The first time I saw a Dungeons and Dragons book I was at a flea market and I thought it looked awesome so I bought them. Except that I thought they were like Choose Your Own Adventure books, and I didn't realize that I would need another person to play it with and this was back in like sixth grade before I had made any friends. Then eventually I met another kid in my middle school who was interested in playing and it was cool, and we started thinking about what the spells would be like if we could cast them in real life, and how we would do it. But then his mom found out and she freaked out because she is Catholic and she thought we were going to become satanists, which is stupid because we were only talking about healing spells, not stuff like Magic Missle.

Nausicaan

Home Planet: ?
Episode: Tapestry
Rating: **

These dudes are not only incredibly ugly, but they are huge assholes as well.
They are basically louder, ruder, angrier Klingons, except instead of always
talking about honor they just act like dicks constantly. What I don't understand is how they are even in outer space. Like, they don't know how to use
prepositions. It seems like using prepositions would be way easier to grasp
than flying a spaceship. Back when Picard was young he fought three of
these aliens, but one of them eventually stabbed him in the heart. Starfleet
people always seem to fight the same way, and it usually very effective. It
seems like some of the other aliens should have figured out a way to do
some counterattacks by now.

Yridian

Home Planet: ?
Episode: Birthright, Pt 1
Rating ***

These aliens look like ugly mole dudes. It is weird, because for most of the show you never hear about these guys but then in the sixth season they start appearing a lot. Another weird thing about them is that the first time we meet one he seems really dumb, it's like he can barely talk better than a Nausicaan, but by the end of the episode his speech seems much more advanced, and then when we see them in the seventh season they talk just like normal people. Nobody in Starfleet seems to trust them, even though they usually follow through on their deals. One of them tries to sell information to Worf that his father is still alive Worf gets really mad about this because he would rather his father be dead than have to deal with the consequences of what it means if he is alive. I can totally understand this. Sometimes I daydream about being an orphan. Like what would happen if my mom was in a car accident or a coma or something. When I think about what my life would be like I think it would be really peaceful. I just imagine that it would feel good to not have to constantly worry all the time about if she is going to to start crying or screaming or treating me like shit. I am so fucking sick of constantly being scared of her. I just want my life to be easy and to live in a house where someone isn't angry or sad all the time. But then I feel bad thinking about it because I it's not like I want her to die, I just want her to not be horrible to me anymore.

Arkarians

Home Planet: Arkaria
Episode: Starship Mine
Rating **

These aliens are pretty generic looking. They are basically humans but with
some extra ridges on their foreheads. It seems like half the aliens the Enterprise meets these day are just humans but with a bumpy nose or forehead
or weird veins or something. Some Arkarians try to steal trilithium resin
when they think that the Enterprise is abandoned, but it turns out that Picard
is also trapped on the Enterprise, and he ends up killing like five people.
Which is crazy. It is not like he cuts their throats, but he repeatedly just
leaves people to die, which is way more hardcore than Picard normally is.
He even shoots someone with a crossbow. Meanwhile there are some other
Arkarians who try to take hostages, and they are basically the worst hostage
takers ever. They just stand around while the hostages make plans for how
they are going to escape and don't do anything about it. Maybe because
there is less crime in the future people are just out of practice. I guess that
is the main thing you should know about Akrarians is that they are criminals, but incompetent criminals, so you don't really need to care about them.
Star Trek always talks about how terrible the Borg are, but at least the Borg
are good at their job.

Ancients

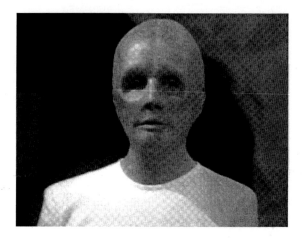

Home Planet: ?
Episode: The Chase
Rating **

These are some aliens that lived billions of years ago before any other aliens
were around. They were lonely and bored and didn't know what else to
do, so they decided to stick their DNA on a bunch of planets so that all the
aliens on those worlds would end up looking like them. Which worked, but
these are like the blandest looking aliens in the universe. They basically
have nothing going on with their heads at all. So I guess that is why so
many aliens look like humans. They are also super selfish, because inside
all these DNAs they somehow hid a computer program that could repro-
gram a tricorder and make a projection of them, which is probably the most
ridiculous thing that has ever been on Star Trek. But also, who the fuck
cares? I think it was a dick move for these aliens to trick the humans and
Cardassians and Romulans and everyone else to run around solving their
stupid puzzle. It's like they were so pathetic and lonely when they were
alive they need to manipulate all the other aliens after they are dead just so
they could make everyone finally pay attention to them.

Tilonians

Home Planet: Tilonus IV
Episode: Frame of Mind
Rating **

These are aliens that have giant foreheads with big ridges on them. Basically it looks like they have McDonalds signs on their heads. Some of these aliens kidnap Riker and torture him for some reason. They basically use a virtual reality machine to make him think he is going crazy. They just keep fucking with him, making him constantly think he is wrong about everything. But then they push him too far and he gets so pissed off that he sees through their bullshit deceptions and breaks out of the machine. There is a band I have started listening to a lot more this year named Tool. Nine Inch Nails is still my favorite band, but Tool is fucking amazing too. They have a song called Bottom and there is a part in it with that guy who sings the Liar song. "If I let you, you would make me destroy myself. But in order to survive you, I must first survive myself. I can sink no further and I cannot forgive you. There's no choice but to confront you, to engage you, to erase you. I've gone to great lengths to expand my threshold of pain. I will use my mistakes against you. There's no other choice. Shameless now. Nameless now. Nothing now. No one now." This song reminds me so much of this episode. Sometimes people push you and they push you and they push you until there is nothing left in you and you hate them so fucking much for it but what they don't realize is how strong your hatred makes you. In this episode Troi tells Riker that he needs to get in touch with his darker side, and he does. He is so filled with darkness that it lets him break their machine and I wish at the end of the episode he took that knife and stabbed the alien in his fucking throat.

Takarans

Home Planet: Takara
Episode: Suspicions
Rating **

In some ways these are like possum aliens, because they can play dead really well, and in some ways they are like starfish aliens, because they don't
have distinct organs, they are all spread out through the body. At one point
Dr. Crusher even shoots this guy in the stomach with a phaser and it burns
a giant hole right through him and he basically doesn't care. They are also
rainbow colored, which is pretty interesting for an alien. But none of these
outweigh that this guy was a huge scumbag. He is a scientist who wants
to steal some technology from another scientist, so he fakes his death, then
he murders the other scientist, then he tries to murder Dr. Crusher. And on
top of that he wants to turn the technology into a weapon. He is an asshole,
because when I hear that someone is a scientist I expect better from them
than stuff like this.

Quantum Singularity Lifeforms

Home Planet: ?
Episode: Timescape
Rating ***

I don't know what to think about these aliens. They incubate their babies
in black holes, which seems really cool. And apparently they are organic
based, but they can still do things like steal other peoples bodies, and live
outside of the timestream, which are normally powers that only an energy
based lifeform would have. These are really impressive abilities. They are
not as good as the powers the Q has, but for the Q it is basically just like
he is casting Wish over and over again, which is cheating, while these guys
are casting Time Stop and Polymorph Self. And both Wish and Time Stop
are ninth level spells, but Wish is supposed to age you five years every time
you cast it, so the way that Q uses it is just totally unrealistic.

Star Trek is interesting because there are a lot of aliens who can do things
that seem like magic but there is a scientific basis for them. I read a quote
once that said that any really advanced technology would look like magic
if you didn't know better. I think this is probably true, which means that
magic could be real, we just need to know how to do it. I need this to be
true. I need to know the missing step that would make magic real. I don't
know what I am going to do about my mom. I am running out of time and
things just get worse and worse every day. There is so much pressure it
makes my heart hurt and pump so fast that I when I am laying in bed I can
feel it shaking the bed. I don't know how I can solve this if magic isn't real.
I need it to be real because if it's not I am going to step into fucking traffic
because no matter what happens it can't be worse than this.

Season Seven

Iyaarans

Home Planet: Iyar
Episode: Liaisons
Rating **

These are even more aliens with bumpy foreheads. These aliens are apparently born fully grown from giant pods, and their food is super bland and they eat only for nutrition, and they don't know anything about love or anger or crime. So they send some ambassadors to the Federation to study these concepts, which is weird. Because they have ships with warp drives, and it's not like the Federation is the first aliens they meet, so you think they would have had plenty of chances to figure out what different foods taste like by now. These aliens are incredibly selfish. One of them tries to trick Picard into falling in love them him by pretending to be a woman who has been trapped on a planet for seven years. She is super needy and manipulative. She sticks a device on Picard that will cause him lots of pain, and that will shock him if he touches it so that he can't leave. She intentionally breaks things then acts pitiful so that Picard will forgive her. But the biggest thing is that she threatens to kill herself in order to make Picard love her, which fucking pisses me off so much, because that is the most shitty thing you can do to someone. I don't understand why my mom does that. If you are scared someone is going to leave you then you should treat them nice, not yell at them or threaten them or tell them you are going to hurt yourself because it is just going to make them hate being around you even more.

Bar Aliens

Home Planet: Various
Episode: Gambit, Pt 1
Rating ***

At the beginning of this episode Riker and Worf and Troi and Crusher are in
a bar, and there are weird aliens that we have never seen before all over the
place. There are way too many to talk about, especially since most of them
don't do anything besides stand around in the background, There is one alien
who is the bartender, and he hits on Troi a lot, but that doesn't make sense to
me. Not only because it is Troi and she is awful, but also because she doesn't
look anything like him. Him thinking Troi is attractive is like if I thought
a monkey is attractive, and I don't. I don't think most monkeys even have
breasts. Another thing that is weird is that Riker and Worf are interrogating
a Yridian about what happened to Picard and he says that Picard got into a
fight with a bunch of aliens, but he says it in a way like Picard wouldn't have
been an alien to him. It's something I don't really understand about Star
Trek, they act like humans are the normal thing and everyone else is an alien,
even though like half the people in the cast aren't humans.

Weird lizard
face alien

Too much hair
alien

Wears a leather
biker jacket in
space alien

Arctus Baran

Home Planet: ?
Episode: Gambit Pt 1
Rating **

This guy is the captain of a ship of mercenaries. He has big hair and a weird forehead. It sort of looks like someone cut a starfish in half and stuck it on his face. Picard talks about how this guy is a shitty captain because he needs to use pain in order to control his crew, but at the same time Baran does manage to assemble an ancient Vulcan weapon that has been lost for two thousand years so it's not like he is super incompetent, he is just a huge asshole. Baran has implanted things in all the people on his ship that lets him instantly cause them pain with a remote control. Eventually Picard leads the crew in a mutiny because he convinces everyone that if they all stand up to Baran together he will have to give in, because he doesn't actually have any power over them except the power they let him have. Which I think is another case of Star Trek being sort of simplistic and self righteous. Because in the real world Boran is a monster, and yeah he can't fly the ship by himself but there are other people on that ship who you care about, and if you try to walk away you don't know know that he isn't going to kill them just because he can. You can't just look out for yourself because then you will be no better than Baran is. In the episode Baran just sort of gives up, but if this was the real world there is no way it would have been that easy. He is used to controlling people with fear and pain and intimidation and there is no way a person like that doesn't hurt people at the end just because he can.

Naric

Home Planet: ?
Episode: Gambit Pt 1
Rating ***

We know this aliens name, but we don't ever find out of the name of his
race of aliens. Which is true of pretty much every alien in this episode, and
that really annoys me. I don't like just writing an aliens first name, it seems
unprofessional. This guy is a mercenary on Arctus Baran's ship. Star Trek
The Next Generation is great, obviously it is my favorite show, but I think
they could make an even better Star Trek show if it was about people who
weren't so goody-goody. Deep Space Nine is sort of like this, but Arctus
Baran and his crew are basically pirates, and I think it would be cool if they
had a Star Trek show about pirates. Most of the other shows I can think of
that have pirates in them have been good: There was a show on a few years
ago called The Pirates of Dark Water, which was awesome, and there was
the show Tale Spin which had pirates in it too. And Tale Spin was probably my favorite of the Disney shows. I mean, Ducktales was really good
too, and that also had pirates on it sometimes. But now there is a new show
called Gargoyles, and I guess it is technically a Disney show even though it
doesn't look anything like Tale Spin or Rescue Rangers or any of the other
ones, and it seems awesome, plus some of the Star Trek people do voices
on it! And this show seems really dark, so I am really looking forward to
when they make more episodes. In general I think the darker a show is,
the better chance it has to be awesome, which is why all the best episodes
of Star Trek are ones like Picard being turned into a Borg, or tortured by
Cardassians, or stuff like that.

Vekor

Home Planet: ?
Episode: Gambit Pt 1
Rating ***

This lady is another one of the mercenaries on Arctus Boran's ship. She had
weird ears and a giant red mohawk and looks awesome. Basically everyone
on that ship looks good, they all look like they could have been in The Road
Warrior, which is a great movie that I rent from the library sometimes. I
don't really care for the first movie in this series, but The Road Warrior and
the third movie are both really good. Even though the good guys who aren't
Mad Max in this movie are basically just wearing football pads that are
falling apart, they look great. They are like futuristic versions of paladins.
Eventually Vekor is killed by a Vulcan lady who is pretending to be a Romulan who found an ancient weapon that lets her kill people by thinking about
it, but what she doesn't realize is that the weapon only works if the victim
was being aggressive. When Picard points this out to her she gets really
depressed and gives up because Picard convinces her the weapon is useless,
which is crazy, because people are still pissed off all the time in the future.
She could just shoot peaceful people with a phaser, and still be able to use the
psychic weapon on aliens like Klingons and Cardassians

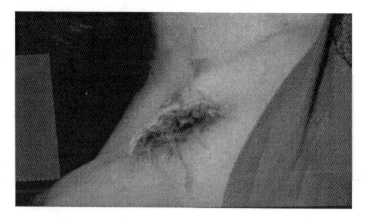

Home Planet: ?
Episode: Phantasms
Rating ***

Even though these aliens are weird creepy mouth things that live on peoples bodies and want to destroy the Enterprise and also suck all the cellular peptides out of people so that they turn into a ball of goo, it is hard for me to dislike them too much because they are responsible for one of the greatest things I have ever seen on the show: Data who is the best character on the show stabs Troi who is the worst character on the show. It is sort of poetic that it happens that way. After he stabs Troi he asks Worf to take care of Spot for him because he is worried that he will go crazy again and hurt Spot too. I cried a little when this happened because it only reinforces how great Data is. Even though he is not supposed to have any emotions he still loves his cat and is super thoughtful about it, while basically Troi is always being selfish and petty, even though she is supposedly the one who is in touch with her emotions.

Cairn

Home Planet: ?
Episode: Dark Page
Rating ***

These aliens are super telepaths. Their telepathic abilities have made their brains so strong that it bulges out in big lumps above their ears. They communicate differently than other telepaths, they just shoot a flood of images at each other, and when they do this they look super intense and pissed off. Also, they have completely forgotten how to talk because their telepathy is so good, so the Federation sends Luxwana to teach them. But it ends up being too much stress for her, plus there is a little alien girl there who reminds her of a daughter she had who died, and the shock of it makes her go into a coma. The Cairn also have a power where they can let Troi walk around in her mom's mind, so they do that so Troi can figure out why her mom went into the coma. Once she does into Luxwana's mind, Luxwana tries to do everything she can to stop Troi, which is fucking stupid, because if she doesn't get help from Troi she is going to die. My mom pulls this shit all the time and it is fucking ridiculous. She just sits there letting her life get worse and worse, and it's like she is trying to punish herself by making her life as horrible as possible, which is a fucked up thing to do because the only person it really hurts is me. And then eventually I have to do stuff and then she gets mad at me for doing the stuff that she refused to do. Fuck her. It is like her mind is filled with fucking poison. There is a book called Dune, they made a movie version of it too which is not as good as the book even though it has Patrick Stewart in it. There are women in the book who are sort of witches, and there is a thing they say, "Fear is the mind killer, fear is the little death that brings total obliteration", and I think that is perfect, because both with Luxwana and my mom they let little bullshit ruin their lives because they are too scared to deal with with it.

Kes/Prytt

Home Planet: Kesprytt
Episode: Attached
Rating *

These aliens come from a world where there are two groups of people. Both of the aliens look the same, basically just humans except they have a small ridge in the middle of their foreheads. But one group of people, the Prytt, are super xenophobic, and the other group of people, the Kes, want to join the Federation. At first we think the Prytt are going to be assholes and the Kes are okay, but then you find out that both of them are fucking stupid. They are both super paranoid, and both think the Federation is plotting with the other group, and Picard and Dr. Crusher almost die because all these aliens are such worthless fuck ups. They just constantly shoot themselves in the foot because they are unwilling to let go of their paranoia and anxiety, which is like the dumbest thing ever. All they have to do is not be paranoid and both groups would be fine, but they can't. They are assholes, and people almost die, and they can't even own up to the fact that it is their fault and maybe if they tried a little fucking harder things wouldn't be so bad, but instead they blame everyone but themselves. They just make things worse and then say it's the Federation's fault that this happened, but it was them. It was them and their fucking immature behavior that ruined everything.

Hekarans

Home Planet: Hekaras II
Episode: Force of Nature
Rating ***

These aliens have really weird forehead creases that make me uncomfortable. I don't know why but they remind me of vaginas. I know that's not what a vagina actually looks like, but still. They seem kind of sexual shaped to me.

Two of aliens who are scientists figure out that using warp drive too much can damage the fabric of space. Lots of ships go by their planet, and if it keeps happening eventually their planet will be destroyed. But the Federation won't listen to them because it would be inconvenient. It seems like people usually don't care very much about the environment, and I think mostly it is because they are lazy and selfish. Last year when I was at a protest I met a guy from a socialist club. I thought it would be pretty cool to join, but it was disappointing. The guy basically said that workers rights were the most important thing, even more than the environment, and I don't think that is always true. What was worse though was that in order for me to join their club I would have to stand around on the street selling their newspapers, which seems like the most boring thing possible, so I quit after three days.

Atreans

Home Planet: Atrea IV
Episode: Inheritance
Rating ***

These are aliens that have giant ears and are weirdly racist against Data.
For the most part the Atrean guy we meet is a pretty normal scientist,
except at one point he starts talking about how they should get a human to
check Data's work because he is only an android. Which is ironic because
it turns out that his wife is not only Data's mom, but she is secretly an android too. A long time ago she died and Dr. Noonian Soong stuck her brain
in an android body, and she doesn't even know she is an android but Data
does, and he is not sure if he should tell her. Data wants to be close to her
even though it was her decision to leave Data behind when the Crystalline
Entity attacked. She said she couldn't deal with having to deactivate Data
like she did Lore when he turned out to be evil. Which is bullshit. It's not
even that she did it because she thought it would have been wrong to kill
Data, she did it because she was too selfish to deal with the guilt. And Data
finally has the chance to have another android to talk to, to not be so lonely
all the time, but he puts her happiness above his. Fuck her. Fuck her for
putting Data to sleep like he was her fucking pet, like she is so much better
than he is. Data is not selfish at all. He gives and gives and gives and in
return all he gets is bullshit like this alien implying he is not as good as a
human.

Boraalan

Home Planet: Boraal II
Episode: Homeward
Rating: ***

Borallans are primitive aliens who lived on a planet that was about to be destroyed because their atmosphere is going to disappear or something. Worf's brother was sent to study them. Then when the planet was going to be destroyed he used the holodeck and the transporter to save one village of them. He said it was because it would be stupid to apply the prime directive in this case, but it was probably just because he had sex with one of the aliens and got her pregnant. Which is weird and fucked up in a lot of different ways. I mean, humans and Boraalans look pretty similar, but their foreheads don't look like human foreheads, so what would he have done if it turned out that his penis didn't look like one of their alien penises? And then when the baby was born the Boraalans would probably figure out something fishy was going on because all of the sudden it is a weird hybrid baby. The most fucked up thing though is that Worf's brother was spying on this woman for a long time before he had sex with her, and also that he is supposed to be a super genius, and she believes in magic and probably has never seen a toothbrush. Him getting married to her would be like getting married to a baby or a caveman. I don't understand how he could stand to be with someone like that.

Home Planet: ?
Episode: Sub Rosa
Rating *

There are a lot of things going on with this alien. His name is Ronin, and he is at least seven hundred years old, and he lives in a candle, and he is made out of anaphasic energy but sometimes he can take human form, and the way he gets food is by having sex with the women in Dr. Crushers family. In a lot of ways this alien is really creepy. First he has sex with her while she is asleep, and then later on he wants to have sex with her and she tells him no but he has sex with her anyways. And since he is invisible there are lots of times where she will just be throwing herself around the room moaning and I guess he is having sex with her while she is doing that. Once Captain Picard watches it happen and it is awkward. It is also weird that the reason this happened is that Beverly's grandmother died, and then she went to the funeral, and afterwards she was reading the diaries of her 100 year old grandmother and how she had lots of sex with Ronin and Beverly was getting turned on by it. I think this is sort of an invasion of her grandmothers privacy, and also it is weird to be aroused by the thought of your grandmother having sex. Oh, and I almost forgot about this, but at one point Ronin takes over the grandmothers dead body and makes her shoot lightning out of her hands. There are a lot of interesting aspects to this alien, but he was still an asshole who raped and manipulated women in Dr. Crushers family for hundreds of years, and also this was probably the worst episode of Star Trek I have ever seen. There are lots of episodes that when they come on in reruns I won't be happy about watching them again because they are not very good, but this is the only one that is so bad that I will just go play video games instead.

Maturin

Home Planet: ?
Episode: Sub Rosa
Rating **

This alien visited Scotland when he was a little kid on vacation with his
family, and he liked it so much that when he grew up he moved to a colony
that was terraformed to feel like Scotland, and eventually he became the
governor of the colony. The thing I don't understand is if he liked Scotland
so much, why didn't he move to the real Scotland and not a fake one? And
why would someone want to make a fake Scotland? If you have the ability
of terraform a place, it seems dumb to just make a place that already exists. Instead they should be making a real life version of Middle-Earth, or
Narnia, or something like that. We already have a Earth, and it's boring.
If it was up to me I would probably make a combination sci-fi and fantasy
planet, where on half the planet there are dragons and centaurs and stuff,
and on the other half there are spaceships so that way there is something for
everyone. Or maybe one with dinosaurs. I don't like dinosaurs nearly as
much as I did when I was younger, but they are still pretty great, and I think
it would be good to be able to visit a planet of them.

Barkonians

Home Planet: Barkon IV
Episode: Thine Own Self
Rating: ***

The Barkonians are sort of a midevil times type of alien. They all have horrible black squiggly lines on their foreheads. A Federation probe crashes on the planet and they send Data to gather the debris because some of it is radioactive, but then there is an accident and Data loses his memory and walks to one of their towns with the radioactive metal and he accidentally poisons a bunch of them. It is weird that because of his amnesia he doesn't remember what the word radioactive means, but he can still say things like interstitial transparency. This episode is basically about how life his horrible. First Data comes to their village and it seems like things might be okay, but then people start getting sick, and no one trusts Data, and then they think he is a monster and hit him in the face with a pickaxe and then when he is trying to save them they stab him in the chest with a giant metal pole and kill him. The people in the village treat Data awful and things just get worse and worse. People tell me my life will get better but they know nothing. Nothing. It can always get worse. It never stops getting worse.

Darsay

Home Planet: Darsay System
Episode: Masks
Rating **

These are aliens who lived millions of years ago. They built a library in space, and then it turned into a comet, then the Enterprise found it and it reprogrammed the Enterprise and also Data. Data was infected with the personalities with people from Darsay mythology, which sucks because all of them had really annoying voices, and acted annoying too. Even though these aliens could build interstellar libraries they still really liked mythology, which is weird. I mean, I like reading books about mythology, but it's not like I believe that that stuff is real. I think once a civilization gets smart enough they should probably stop thinking that the sun is a god, especially if they have spaceships. You can tell that Data is really freaked out by the situation, because he knows things about the aliens that he shouldn't know, and then Geordi is running a diagnostic and something snaps in Data and he asks Geordi what it feels like to lose ones mind and that is when the other personalities take over. Losing your mind is something I think about a lot. There are lots of times that I get furious at my mom for the way she acts but there are also lots of times that I just feel... I don't know. I feel overwhelmed and panicky because I know that things are about to get worse and there is nothing I can do to stop it. And when this happens I just start constantly thinking about doing things like jumping out of a window or falling down the stairs or taking a bottle and breaking it and using the shards to cut up my face. I cut my arms and my legs sometimes, but that is different. I can control when I do that, and it helps me feel better. But this other stuff feels like I am falling apart and I am not going to be able to stop myself when it finally happens and that really scares me. I hate my life. I should not have to feel this.

Nara

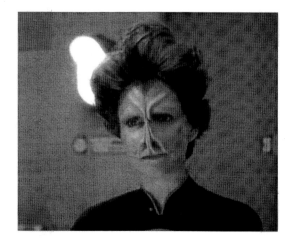

Home Planet: ?
Episode: Eye of the Beholder
Rating ***

This aliens has a weird looking forehead, but it's not nearly as fucked up as her nose. I think having a crazy nose is basically the worst thing that you can have if you're an alien. There are lots of aliens that are still hot even if they have forehead bumps, or weird spots, or even if they are different colors, but aliens with weird noses are almost never attractive, especially if it means there is something wrong with their nostrils. In this episode Troi starts hallucinating because she stands too close to a spot where someone committed suicide once. While she is hallucinating she imagines that she and Worf have sex, which is like the least plausible thing that has ever happened on this show. Worf has always been attracted to strong women and Troi is basically just a snivelling little child in an adult's body. She is fucking worthless and miserable and it is utterly ridiculous that he would want to have sex with her.

Napeans

Home Planet: ?
Episode: Eye of the Beholder
Rating: *

Fuck her. Fuck her so much. I don't deserve this. I fucking hate her more
than anything and I don't know how I can bear this. I am going to explode. I
want her to die. I want us to both die. I just got home from school and
my mom was in the kitchen and she was screaming about how much she
hated her life and she was breaking all the dishes and when I tried to stop
her she hit me. I don't know what to do. Fuck her. I am so furious at her
and I am scared and FUCK HER. I fucking hate myself so much. I don't
understand why I can't walk away from her. She is so fucking horrible
and I hate her and I know if I leave home she is just going to kill herself. I
fucking hate this. I hate my life. It shouldn't be like this. I know I wont
leave her because if I leave she will commit suicide and I hate myself so
much for being weak cause she wins. She fucking wins again and I hate
this I hate this I hate this I hate this I hate this. I am going to explode. She
is a monster and I wish I could let her die. I am so fucking weak and stupid
and I can't do this anymore.

Dopterians

Home Planet: ?
Episodes: Firstborn
Rating: *

Fuck these aliens. They are just rip off Ferengis. They are greedy and snivelling and liars. Their heads are even similar. I don't know why I am even
bothering with this shit if they are going to be so uncreative with their aliens.
If they are not going to care, if they are not going to try, then fuck them. I
feel like I am eating up every good thing inside me just to keep myself from
exploding. I am done with this.

Enterprise AI

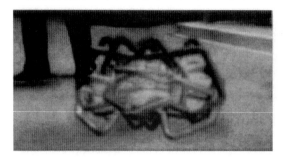

Home Planet: Enterprise
Episodes: Emergence
Rating: ***

I know what I have to do. I look back at these aliens, and I see now the answer repeating itself again and again. The ambassador who puts his negative energy into Troi. Riker goes crazy and keeps jumping between different realities. Data has multiple personalities. Luxwana walls off part of her mind. And then especially this episode. This episode is the one that really gave me the idea. The Enterprise computer is so powerful, and has seen so much stuff, that it starts to become conscious. But it is still stuck being the computer, so it starts to make a new version of itself that can explore the galaxy. There is some dumb stuff with the holodeck and a train, but eventually it works. In one of the entries for the other aliens I mentioned a thing that happened in an issue of Sandman where a guy knew something horrible was going to happen, so he tore his shadow from his body and gave it life, and he told it "my death is now your death, and my doom your doom. Yours and yours alone, my shadow." This is what I will do. I am going to tear my shadow from my body. I know I will never be able to leave my mom. Even after all the bullshit she has done to me I am still too weak to walk away from her. I wish I didn't feel guilt, or responsibility, but I do. I hate myself so much for not being strong enough to leave her. So I'm stuck, but there is still a way to escape. I am going to cut away at myself until I make another me. A little version of myself and when things get bad I will pour into him all my hate and sorrow and anger and frustration. He will suffer, and I will feel nothing, and I will be perfect like Data. This is my goal. I have a knife and my flesh and my will and magic and I will make this work.

ALIENS FROM THE MOVIES

(OR ACCIDENTALLY
OMITTED FROM THE
ORIGNAL ZINES)

Minosian

Home Planet: Minos
Episode: The Arsenal of Freedom
Rating: **

This is a race of aliens that look like incredibly prolific character actors. I don't know who this guy is, but I know I've seen him in a lot of things. The Minosians were arms merchants, and people on the Enterprise act scandalized that they once sold arms to both sides of a civil war. A short time earlier all signs of life disappeared from the planet, and the Enterprise is sent to investigate it. They discover that they were killed by one of their own weapons, but nobody seems very upset about the fact that most likely millions if not billions of people just died. That they are standing upon the tomb of an entire species and have no emotional response other than being mildly irritated that the alien weapon is trying to kill them now too. The other thing that really bugged me about these aliens, and I can remember it bothering me even as a kid, is that aliens who have developed civilization-destroying super weapons should also have the technology to construct roads and buildings. But no, these people apparently just hung out in the jungle, and their main staging area for weapons operations is a thirty foot pit that doesn't even have a ladder.

Tkonian

Home Planet: Tkon
Episode: The Last Outpost
Rating: ***

These aliens all died out 600,000 years ago, and if the immortal
guardian they set to patrol the outskirts of their empire is any indication, they all looked like a wax museum replicas of Emperor Palpatine
who've started to melt. Also the guy has a halberd, which I'm pretty
sure is not a weapon that exists outside of the Dungeons and Dragons player handbook. Which is weird: if these aliens had an empire
encompassing trillions of people with the ability to move entire star
systems, the best weapon they can come up with is a halberd? If
anything this guy should be using a glaive guisarme. This guy seems
pretty condescending, and is really excited to talk to Riker about
Sun Tzu. In my experience any time you meet someone over the age
of 16 who is into Sun Tzu it's a big red flag that they're going to be
insufferable.

Riker's Jazz Band Alien

Home Planet: Unknown
Episode: Second Chances
Rating: ***

This is some alien playing keyboards in Riker's jazz band. We don't
know anything about him other than he has a melty face. It really
bothered me as a kid what boring taste everyone on Star Trek has
in music. It was always classical or jazz. I wanted someone to like
Nine Inch Nails. Or even listen to music from the future. But no,
everyone on Star Trek has a big hardon for Mozart and Shakespeare.
You would think in a world where they have eliminated the need for
money or want there would be a lot of people making art, but apparently none of them can make anything better than 400 year old
generic jazz music.

Delbians

Home Planet: Delb II
Episode: The Drumhead
Rating: **

Another incredibly boring alien that looks like a human except with
a slightly bumpier forehead. At least she has some weird Bjork hair
buns. I always hated writing stuff for aliens like this. It seemed
dumb to include ones like this that barely even get a speaking part,
but I did want the guide to be as complete as possible. On the other
hand it was hard to draw the line between this, and aliens you see
in the background that I would have no idea what to say about, or
non-sentient aliens like that killer plant that attacked Riker in the clip
show episode. Whatever. These aliens are good at standing around
apparently, because that's pretty much all she ever does.

Mr. Homn

Home Planet: Unknown
Episode: Haven
Rating: ***

This guy is Laxwana Troi's slave butler guy. He is very tall and strong.
He rarely talks. He basically has no personality except for the fact
that he steals drinks a lot, which is probably the only thing that
makes being Laxwana's slave bearable. Also, I didn't realize it until
looking at this picture just now, but Patrick Stewart is basically a tiny
version of him.

Marinjian

Home Planet: Subspace
Episode: Interface
Rating: **

Another in a long line of subspace assholes. Anytime you
meet an alien who lives in subspace it is pretty safe to assume
they are a jerk. These aliens look like floating balls of fire,
which is the only good thing about them. They live in the
atmosphere of a gas giant and get trapped on Geordi's mom's
ship. They accidentally murder the entire crew trying to get
out, and then when Geordi shows up they attempt to contact
him too, despite knowing the high probability Geordi would
also be killed in the process. Then they manipulate him into
thinking his mom is really alive, fooling him into saving
them despite it putting Geordi in mortal peril. Normally
this is where I would've spelled out some parallel with my
mom treating me shitty, but you get the idea by now.

Ba'ku

Home Planet: Ba'ku
Episode: Star Trek: Insurrection
Rating: *

The Baku are a race of extremely bland, self-righteous aliens who are basically indistinguishable from the people in an LL Bean catalog. Hundreds of years ago they were flying around in spaceships like everyone else, but then a small group of them thought that their civilization was about to collapse so they hid on a planet that has a fountain of youth effect. Now they just sit around making quilts and judging people who actually do something with their lives, even though the only way they can maintain their lifestyle is because their planet is magic. Then Picard shows up and is captivated by their culture of doing fuck-all for centuries at a time, which is ridiculous because a) this is the exact opposite of everything that Picard is and believes in, and b) It has been established that there is no shortage of colonies that lead a laid-back, agrarian existence. It's not like this is a novel way of existence that Picard wouldn't have encountered before. Lots of people live this way. Hell, that's basically the whole deal with Risa, except there they also have constant fucking.

Son'a

Home Planet: Ba'ku
Episode: Star Trek: Insurrection
Rating: **

These are the bad guys of the movie. They used to be Baku, then one hundred years ago they rebelled and the Baku kicked them off the planet, although the Baku are supposed to be strict pacifists and the Sona aren't, so I'm not sure how they accomplished that. Then I guess not being on the planet caused their bodies to get all fucked up, which lends an interesting angle to the Baku lady trying to get Picard to stay: if he stays he will become dependant on the planet and turn into a monster if he tries to leave. Anyways, even though there are only 600 Baku on their entire planet and the Sona were a smaller group that tried to break away, there are somehow enough of them that they have created a civilization that built and maintains a military that spans several systems in only the past century. Which... whatever, fine. It's not like the tv shows were possessing of ironclad logic and free of plot holes. But this is so ridiculous to be insulting.

Evora

Home Planet: Evora
Episode: Star Trek: Insurrection
Rating: ***

The Evora are short aliens that look like turtles and don't realize that
the floral centerpieces at the fancy reception are decoration and not
food. Ha ha, get it? They are different than us, and therefore a joke!
Everything about them is a fucking joke! They put a goofy bead
thing on Picard's head! HAHAHA! I had a fucked up childhood.
You know that. And one of the things that gave me hope that the
world could be better was Star Trek. But it is hard for me to watch as
an adult because despite having these messages of egalitarianism and
inclusion, the racism of the people who made the show so obviously
bleeds through. TNG helped me a lot, but it's also hard not to be
disappointed or angry at shit like this. Despite all their claims otherwise, the Star Trek and the Federation represents the beautiful and the
powerful and the rich, and they look down on anyone different than
themselves.

Tarlac

Home Planet: Tarlac
Episode: Star Trek: Insurrection
Rating: ***

I guess they're supposed to be cosmeticians, but also slaves? They seem to smile a lot for people who are enslaved, but I can fucking goddamn attest that a lot of the time it's easier just to smile and nod and put up with someone's bullshit than it is to fight back. There will be times in your life that you think things are bad, but it's important to keep in mind how much worse they could be. The Tarlac seem like nice enough people, and the Sona are psychopaths. When you are in a situation like this, you need to recognize what your opponent is capable of. If you are going to resist then you need to be willing to match their anger and darkness and crazy beat for beat. If you can't do that then just keep your head down and eat shit. Try and fail, or don't try at all. Either way in the end your heart is going to scab over a little. But if you try and fail it will be much, much worse.

Ellora

Home Planet: Ellora
Episode: Star Trek: Insurrection
Rating: ***

I don't really know what to say about these aliens. I guess they look sort of like a Triceratops because they have giant foreheads? Honestly, until I started reading about the movie on the internet I had no idea that these guys weren't just Sona that looked different. I mean, the whole thing with the Sona is that they are weird looking, so that seems like an easy mistake to make. But no, this is another race of slaves. I don't know what to say about them. Honestly, I wouldn't even have the Triceratops thing except that it mentioned it on their wiki page. These zines would have been much easier to write if the internet was around back then. Oh, here is a thing about them: the makup for the women of this species is different than the males because they didn't want it to interfere with their hotness. Good job, Star Trek producers. Good job being sexist fucking hypocrites.

Kolarans

Home Planet: Koralus III
Episode: Star Trek Nemesis
Rating: **

The important lesson about these aliens is that there is nothing in this
world good enough that someone else can't ruin it. I thought that
nothing in the Star Trek universe could ever be worse than Voyager,
but this movie proved me wrong. These are scaly aliens that live on a
desert planet driving around in some Mad Max dune buggies. Then
Picard comes down, despite this civilization being pre-warp and this
being a violation of the prime directive. Also, he isn't supposed to go
on away missions, especially if there are a bunch of violent aliens and
a giant storm that's about to hit. Whatever. Picard drives around in
his own dune buggy hooting like an asshole, and the Kolarans shoot
at him because from their perspective aliens have invaded their planet
and started stealing their collection of hidden android body parts
(and it is never explained why these are scattered on the planet). So
then Data and Worf try to murder the aliens with phasers, with no
regard to the thought that maybe these aliens are just freaked out and
scared and have children at home who love them. But no, they have
fucked up faces so it is okay to murder them with impunity.

INTERVIEW WITH JOSHUA CHAPMAN
RECORDED FEBRUARY 23, 2016, DORMONT, PENNSYLVANIA

ZACH: First off, I just want to say thank you so much for doing this.

JOSHUA: Okay.

I mean it. Writing the zines, allowing us to collect them, doing this interview, everything.

Yeah, okay.

Alright, lets get started with the big question: Do you still watch Star Trek?

Sometimes. I haven't lately. I watched a lot of them a few years ago when they came on Netflix.

Have you seen the new movies? What did you think of them?

They're okay. They're sort of a betrayal of everything that Star Trek is supposed to stand for, so you know, that sucks. But at least they're not as bad as the prequel Star Wars movies.

Are you a Star Wars fan? What do you think about Star Wars versus Star Trek?

Star Wars is fine. I never cared about it like I did Trek, but I enjoyed them.

I mean, what do you think about how there is almost a competition between them in geek culture? That people can't like both of them?

It's dumb? Most geek culture is fucking stupid. It's like, they claim to be misunderstood outcasts while the making the central pillar of their subculture the most popular movie of all time. They might as well base their alienation on liking ice cream.

(laughs) Which is your favorite Star Trek alien?

Cardassians.

Really? I thought for sure you would say Data, or maybe the Vulcans. You didn't even give the Cardassians five stars in your zines.

Data and the Vulcans, they represented an escape for my adolescent self that I don't need anymore, or at least not in that way. Cardassians, on the other hand, are like the closest thing to actual people in the Star

Trek universe. They get to be interesting and flawed in a way most of the aliens in Star Trek don't get to be. They get to be complex. Plus Garak from *Deep Space Nine* was great.

Can I ask you how you got the pictures of all the aliens for your zines? It had to be difficult to do in an era before the internet.

Not really. I taped all the episodes when they came on, and when I was making the zines I'd just put in the appropriate tape, pause it at the right moment and take a polaroid of the TV.

Okay, shifting gears, tell me a little bit about yourself. Are you married? Do you have kids?

No and no.

What about your mom? Do you still talk to her at all?

(Pauses) Yeah, I really don't want to talk about that.

Okay, fair enough, I know that must be a difficult topic for you. So, do you often think about the zines? Do you ever re-read them?

I don't. I don't think I even have copies anymore.

Would you be interested in reading them again?

No, not really. I have too many memories of my childhood already. I don't need to dredge up more.

What happened after the end of the final issue?

What do you mean?

Well, things seemed very grim for you. You were obviously extremely unhappy and angry and unsure of your future. And I have to admit, I've never completely understood the ending.

Well, you don't really need to. I didn't write it for you.

Who did you write it for?

I wrote it for me not bashing my head against the corner of the coffee table. I wrote it so that I'd have something to do after school besides getting drunk on mouthwash.

Shit, um... okay. Can I ask what happened after the last issue? Did things get better for you?

I graduated high school. And no, not really, no. Why would they? Bad things are going to happen. It's like, people have this idea that once they get past some obstacle in their life, there will be good things waiting on the other side, but... That's not life. In life, you get past bullshit, and then there's just some new kind of bullshit waiting for you.

Does it help at all to know that twenty years later, people are still enjoying these zines you wrote as a kid?

Yeah, I'm real happy they are getting a kick out of my shitty childhood and how sad I was all the time.

I assume you're kidding?

Well, yeah. It's just, you were talking before we started the interview about how you would do readings of my zines, and people in the crowd laughing, and I feel like they must not understand what the point of me writing them was. What they really meant.

What did people think of your zines back then? What sort of feedback did you get when you were making them?

Basically none. Like, at the time, almost no one besides my teachers saw the first two issues. I think I gave the third issue out to some friends in school, and they told me it was funny, but I don't think they recognized it for what it was. But I guess neither did I. It wasn't until maybe the fourth issue that I figured out why making them was important for me.

So what did you do then?

I stopped giving them out at school because I didn't want to risk them getting back to my teachers or my mom. I was leaving them at record stores, mostly. Some of the cashiers told me that people were curious about the early issues and asked me to reprint them, so I did. But I never included any contact information in them, and I stopped giving them out to anyone I knew personally, so once I dropped them off I never heard back about them again.

Why keep writing them if no one you knew would read them?

(Shrugs) Cause I was in an abusive relationship and I needed to talk about it and it was the only safe way I felt I could.

Okay, you said a word there I have been reluctant to use when describing your zines because I didn't want to place any judgments on your relationship with your mom: abuse. You would describe the relationship as abusive?

That's... a tricky question. But also like,

yeah, absolutely. We have this idea that someone who is an abuser, they do it because they are evil, or controlling. But eventually, I realized that my mom wasn't treating me the way she was because she hated me, or she was trying to hurt me. There's just something that went wrong in her, and it makes her act the way she does. But I don't think she likes being that way. She doesn't get pleasure from it. It's like… just because you need someone to love you doesn't mean they have it in them to do so, and just because someone doesn't mean to hurt you doesn't make it hurt any less when they do. It's more complicated than we like to think of those situations being, but that didn't make it not abuse.

It sounds like part of you feels sorry for her.

Yeah, sometimes, of course I do. She didn't choose this. She's the most unhappy person I've ever met. But at the same time it's something I really struggle with. Because there have been times that when I have pitied her and I've hated myself for it afterward. Cause it feels like I'm trying to justify the way she treated me. I can recognize that she acts the way she does because she has problems, and that she's suffering, too. But, imagine a woman crying cause her husband beat her for burning dinner, and him saying to her, "I don't know what you're so upset about, I'm

the one who suffers from violent rages." There have been times that I've hated myself for not being a better son, not doing more to make sure she gets help, and for not loving her enough to forgive her. But no one would expect a wife to try and sympathize with why her husband hits her. Having her emotions so out of control is scary for her, but after awhile, I don't care any more than I care if the needles hurt the cactus. It's enough that the needles hurt me.

I can't help but notice you're using present tense a lot when talking about your mom.

(Sighs) Yeah.

Are you…?

I still live with her, yeah.

Oh! That wasn't what I was going to ask at all. Really?

Yeah.

I… I didn't expect that.

(Shrugs) Neither did I eighteen years ago. But here we are.

Are you okay with that?

No. I accept it, for lack of a better word.

Are things... different? I mean, a lot of time has passed. You're both a lot older.

No, things are pretty much the same as they were. I mean, yes, things are different because I'm better at processing her shit now, and I'm more able to not to take it personally, but my mom hasn't changed.

So, is it not so bad anymore?

Sometimes it's okay. It was always okay sometimes, even when I was making the zines. I always have to be mindful, and sort of walk on eggshells around her, but she can go weeks at a time and be fine. But, then sometimes she's not, and when it gets bad it's still very horrible. She poisons the air we breathe with her bullshit. It's like when the army captures someone and they make them listen to death metal so they can't sleep or think or do anything.

How do you deal with that? It sounds... unbearable.

I'm used to it. I don't know. I'm used to it. A lot of it is… if I can get away, I'll just go have a drink in a bar. Or get a slice of pizza. Just something boring. A big part of living with someone like my mom is that most of the time you don't really get to have emotions or needs, so when things are bad after awhile I stop feeling like I'm a real person. It can be important to just do

something normal. It helps, but I don't think I could explain to you why.

Do you have anyone who helps you with this stuff? I know before you said you weren't married...

No. I don't want to bring another person into my life. It wouldn't be fair to them. And I am… not good about that stuff. It took me a long time to realize, but… I don't know. I'm angry pretty much all the time. I don't want to do to someone else what she's done to me.

If she's still treating you this way, why do you still stay with her?

Cause if I left she could die. Or, maybe if I stayed she'll get better. She wasn't always like this, you know. She could get better. And if I could help make that happen, but it didn't happen because I left, then... I don't know. I don't know. She's my mom. She's still my mom. As much as I hate her sometimes I don't... You need to... (sighs) This is so humiliating. This is so fucking humiliating. You have no idea what it's like to love someone and know that everyone thinks you're stupid for it. To know how you're a disappointment to everyone in your life because you let someone treat you a certain way.

I don't...
Yes you do. Yes you do. Every single time

there is something in the news about a woman getting abused, like Rihanna or that football player's wife, all I hear is (mocking tone) "Why does she stay with him? That's not what I would do." No idea. People have no fucking idea.

That seems...

Okay, stop. I'm not strong enough. That's what it boils down to. I'm a coward no matter what I do, and I've had to face that every day for like twenty years now. I mean… I could leave her. I know that's an option. But at this point it actually feels harder for me to walk away, you know? Sometimes I wish I was selfish enough to leave, I really do. I know that sounds fucked up, like I'm trying to make myself out to be a saint for staying, but that's really not it at all. I do wish I could leave. I wish.… (long pause) You know, I still think about being hit by cars? That is one thing I remember putting in the zines. How great it would be to have a car slam into me, and put me in a coma, and then I would wake up with a new life without having to take responsibility for leaving my mom. Every single day I still think about that. I–I don't expect you to understand, okay? It's just, I know I can bear any bullshit she puts me through. I've been doing this a long time. But, I'm scared I can't bear what might happen if I left. I shouldn't owe her anything, but I do, and I don't expect you to understand. (long pause) This, this is why I said I didn't want

to talk about her before, and I don't blame you, I know I was the one who brought her up. But I've had this conversation so, so many times and… I'm tired of feeling like a disappointment to people. (pauses) I'm sorry. I know you came a long way for this, but can we be done?

No, of course, that's fine. I was almost at the end of the questions anyways. Would it be okay if I asked you one more? A friend asked me to ask you this, and I would hate to leave it off.

Sure.

Great. And thank you again so much for letting us republish your zines, and for taking the time to do this interview. Alright, last question: If you could go back in time and say one thing to your teenage self, what would it be?

(Pauses) Give up hope. Things would have been so much easier if I had accepted earlier on that my life wasn't going to get better. I kept wanting my mom to be someone she was no longer capable of being. The constant disappointment was the worst part. That's what I would tell myself. Life will never get better, and it will hurt less when you accept that.

INDEX

ZACHARY AUBURN

is the author of *How to Talk to Your Cat About Gun Safety*,
*Love Is Not Constantly Wondering if You Are Making
the Biggest Mistake of Your Life*,
My Complicated Relationship with Food,
and is co-author of *Miami, You've Got Style:
A Little Golden Girls Book*.
He lives in Rochester, New York.
For more, visit zacharyauburn.com.

JOSHUA CHAPMAN

lives in Dormont, Pennsylvania.
He has asked not to be contacted.

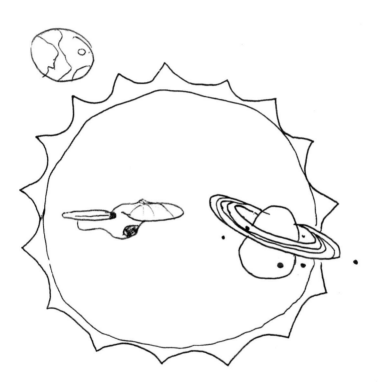

READ MORE FUNNY BOOKS FROM

THE DEVASTATOR

- ☐ **All the Feelings** by M.F.A. Levine, MFA
- ☐ **At Least You're Not These Monsters**
      by Danny Lacy and Mike Levine
- ☐ **Best American Emails** by Amanda Meadows
- ☐ **The Devastator (Anthology Series)** by Various
- ☐ **Dream It! Screw It!** by Geoffrey Golden
- ☐ **Frankenstein's Girlfriend** by Geoffrey Golden
- ☐ **Grosslumps: Tales to Irritate Your Spook Glands**
      by P.F. Chills
- ☐ **Killing It** by Joan Ford
- ☐ **Oh, the Flesh You Will Eat!** by Dr. Vireuss
- ☐ **The Presidential Dickerbook** by Patrick Baker
- ☐ **Restart Me Up** by Lesley Tsina
- ☐ **Snarkicide** by Geoffrey Golden
- ☐ **Stay at Home Scarface** by Kenny Keil
- ☐ **Toys "4" Cheap**
      by Asterios Kokkinos and Jimmy Hasse
- ☐ **We Don't Think You're Racist!**
      by Amanda Meadows and Robin Higgins
  Wet Hot American Summer: Fantasy Camp RPG
      by Geoffrey Golden and Lee Keeler

ᴅEVASTATORPRESS.COM